The BIG BAD WOLF MURDER

For my brother, Chris

First published in the UK in 2025 by Usborne Publishing Limited, Usborne House, 83-85 Saffron Hill, London EC1N 8RT, England, usborne.com

Usborne Verlag, Usborne Publishing Limited, Prüfeninger Str. 20, 93049 Regensburg, Deutschland, VK Nr. 17560

Text copyright © Ty Gloch Limited, 2025.

The right of P. G. Bell to be identified as the author of this work has been asserted by him in accordance with the Copyright, Designs and Patents Act, 1988.

Cover and inside illustrations by George Ermos © Usborne Publishing Limited, 2025.

The name Usborne and the Balloon logo are Trade Marks of Usborne Publishing Limited

All rights reserved. No part of this publication may be reproduced or used in any manner for the purpose of training artificial intelligence technologies or systems (including for text or data mining), stored in retrieval systems or transmitted in any form or by any means without prior permission of the publisher.

This is a work of fiction. The characters, incidents, and dialogues are products of the author's imagination and are not to be construed as real. Any resemblance to actual events or persons, living or dead, is entirely coincidental.

A CIP catalogue record for this book is available from the British Library.

ISBN 9781836040743   10005/1   JFMAM JASOND/25

Printed and bound in Great Britain by CPI Group (UK) Ltd, Croydon, CR0 4YY.

The BIG BAD WOLF MURDER

P.G. BELL

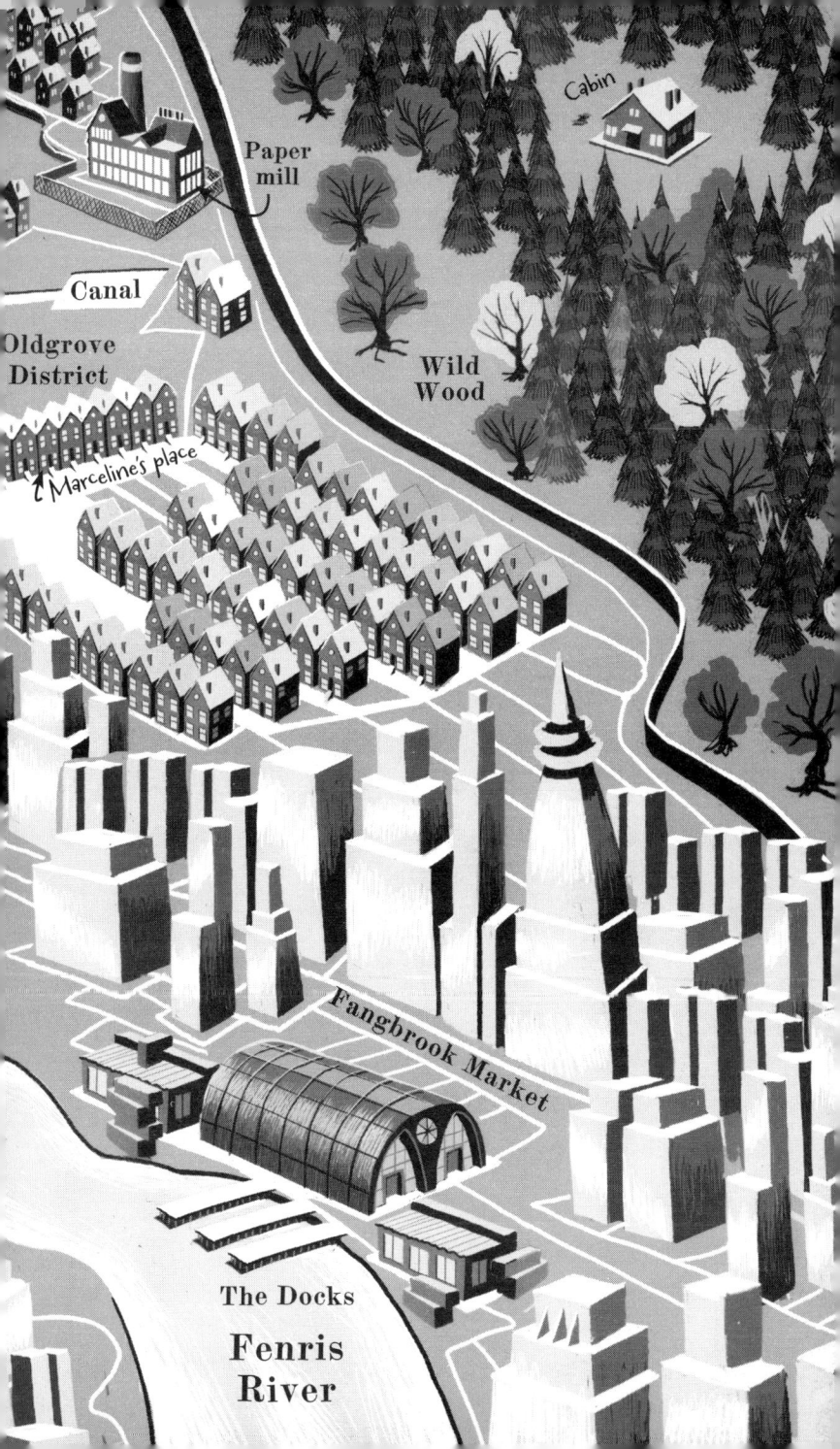

CHAPTER 1
Game Time

Ruby was being hunted. The thrill of it ran through her veins like fire, making her skin prickle and her muscles tense as she darted from bush to bush. Their paper leaves tickled her face, and she paused to pluck a bright pink silk flower from one of them. It was soaked in perfumed oils, and she smiled as she rubbed it over her tracksuit.

Good luck tracking my scent now, she thought.

Nevertheless, she looked around, alert to any movement. Cartoon bluebirds smiled down at her from flat cardboard trees. And rising beyond the fake forest in every direction was the crowd, row upon row of people, watching in silence.

Fifty thousand spectators were crammed into the stands of Netherburg Stadium, but it seemed that every one of them was holding their breath. That told Ruby the danger was close – the hunter was closing in, and they were waiting for him to strike.

The soft hoot of a wood pigeon came from the trees behind her. Not daring to blink, she cupped her hands around her mouth and returned the call. A second later, a small figure in red stepped out from cover. It was her teammate, Akako – fifteen, with a compact, muscular frame, her black hair packed in a bun. She signalled to Ruby in a rapid series of hand gestures. *Any sign?*

Ruby signalled back. *No, but—*

She didn't have time to react to the huge shadow that reared up behind Akako. Yellow eyes blazed in its depths, there was a flash of white teeth, and two large grey-furred hands plucked Akako from her feet. In barely a second, she was gone.

Ruby turned and ran. The crowd leaped to their feet, roaring with excitement, but not even their combined voices could drown out the low, animal howl from the trees behind her.

She ran faster, vaulting onto a narrow balance beam across a water trap, then leaping to grab a rope that hung from a nearby tree. She swung across a web of netting spread on the ground to trip the unwary, then dropped, rolled, and burst out of the forest into a circular clearing.

"Ruby!" The team captain, Roselyn, was waiting for her. Even in the middle of a game, she looked glamorous – eighteen years old, willowy, with ash-blond hair and an unflinching gaze. The exact opposite of Ruby, who was small, wiry and pale, with black hair scraped back from a wide forehead. "Where is he?"

"Behind me," Ruby panted, backing away from the treeline.

"And Akako?"

"Out," said Ruby. "What about Voss?"

"He got her too," said Roselyn. "But not before we both got our flags up."

They reached the centre of the clearing, where four flagpoles stood. Red flags flew from two of them. The others were bare.

"Mine makes three," said Ruby, unfolding an identical flag from a pouch on her belt.

"I'll raise it," said Roselyn. "You keep watch."

Ruby handed her the flag and turned to scan the trees. Nothing stirred, but she knew the hunter had to be close. He would be watching.

Three flags, she thought. *We can still win this.*

Tooth & Claw was a simple game. A team of four runners had to negotiate the arena's obstacles, reach the clearing in the centre, and raise their flags without being caught by the hunter. Five points for each flag raised, and five more for each player who made it back through the forest to safety. They only needed twenty points to win, and her flag gave them fifteen already. If she or Roselyn could escape the forest, the final five points were theirs, and so was the championship. The soles of her feet itched with anticipation.

"Any sign of him?" asked Roselyn as the flag reached the top of the pole. The crowd cheered wildly in support.

"None," Ruby replied. "But he's here. I know it."

The two girls stood back to back, unblinking.

"We'll split up," said Roselyn. "He can only catch one of us."

"I'll go north," said Ruby.

"I'll take south," said Roselyn. "On three. One…"

"Three!" yelled Ruby, sprinting for the underbrush. She dismissed the faint twinge of guilt at not waiting for Roselyn's countdown – the scoring line was out there, just out of sight. But so was the hunter, and even as she took her first steps, some instinct warned her that she was heading into a trap. She veered hard right, now running east. At the same instant, a huge shaggy shape erupted from the bushes to the north, fangs bared. She felt its claws brush the back of her ponytail as it sailed past her. She powered on, not daring to look back.

As she reached the cover of the trees, she heard Roselyn scream. Then came that terrible howl again, and another almighty cheer from the crowd.

Five points left, she thought as the blood hammered in her ears. *I have to do this.*

She was the last player standing. The hunter was on her tail, but she had a head start. That would be enough as long as nothing—

Her foot caught on a hidden tripwire, and she landed flat on her face. Panic squeezed the breath from her lungs, and she rolled to one side an instant before the hunter surged past in a whirl of teeth and claws.

The crowd fell silent again as Ruby sprang to her feet and came face to face with him. The big bad wolf.

He padded back and forth on all fours, as large as a lion, his muzzle dripping saliva and his yellow eyes gleaming with triumph.

"Hello again, Ruby." His voice was as deep and thick as mud.

"Alarick," she replied. "Looks like it's just you and me."

He reared onto his hind legs, over two metres of muscle wrapped in salt-and-pepper fur. "The best of the best," he said. "That's why I saved you until last."

"You didn't save me for anything," she shot back. "I'm just too quick for you."

He smiled, revealing more long, curved teeth. "We'll see."

The edge of the arena was barely twenty metres behind him. So close! Ruby feinted left, darted right, but he dropped to all fours again, flowing as quickly and smoothly as oil to block her. He snapped his jaws and laughed.

"Too obvious," he said. "Try again."

Her frustration sparked into anger – he was toying with her. "I meant what I told you earlier," she said. "I'm going to win this. For Marceline."

His smile faded. "She doesn't need you to settle her old scores." He raised his head to survey the crowd for an instant, and Ruby wondered if this was her chance to slip around him. But he was cunning, and she knew this was almost certainly a trick.

Sure enough, the moment passed and he locked eyes with her again. "Give me your best shot," he said. "It's time to pay my dues."

A growl built in his throat, and Ruby dropped into a sprinter's crouch. This was it. Alarick would lunge and she would spring clear. But which way? Get it right, and she could reach safety before he had time to turn and catch her. Get it wrong, and the five points went up in smoke.

She tensed...but the attack never came. Instead, Alarick's growl turned into a wet gurgle, and he put his paws to his throat. Was this another trick? "Just come at me," she snapped.

He didn't answer but reared up again, staggering from side to side. The watching crowd gave a murmur of disquiet.

Ruby made up her mind and bolted, expecting Alarick's paws to close around her at any second. When they didn't, she risked a look back. He turned to her with wide, desperate eyes. She stumbled to a halt.

"Alarick?"

With a last, choking cough, he toppled onto his back.

Ruby stood, frozen in shock until a trio of medics – two humans, one wolf – hurried past her. She stumbled after them as they set about checking Alarick's pulse, shining a penlight into his eyes, and starting chest compressions.

This couldn't be happening. She had spent months – years! – training to beat Alarick. And here he was, staring blindly at the sky as a trail of white foam oozed from his maw onto the turf.

"Is he all right?" she asked, realizing what a silly question it was as soon as she said it. She didn't need the chief medic's weary shake of the head to know the answer. Alarick was dead.

CHAPTER 2
Locker Room Talk

Ruby's teammates swarmed her the second she stepped into the locker room.

"Is it true?" said Voss. She was stocky and square, her wavy red hair flopping into her face as she bounced nervously from foot to foot. "Is Alarick really…?"

"He can't be," said Akako, throwing a supportive arm around Ruby. "What happened out there, Rubes?"

Ruby tried to answer, but she was still fighting to make sense of it all. One second Alarick had been alive, daring her to beat him, and the next…

A hand grabbed her shoulder and spun her around. It was Roselyn.

"Never mind Alarick," she said. "Did you get the points?"

Ruby blinked in shock, then shook her head.

"What?" Roselyn threw her hands up. "You had a clear run to the boundary!"

"I know!" Ruby replied. "And I was almost there, but then Alarick..." She remembered the look in the wolf's eyes as he'd collapsed. He had looked *scared*. "I had to turn back."

"Alarick's the enemy," said Roselyn. "We've been training all year to beat him – to humiliate him! – and you blew it."

"Go easy, Ros," said Akako, only to be silenced by a warning glare.

Ruby's anger flared. "I hated him as much as you did, but that's not the same as wanting him dead." She turned to Voss for support, but her teammate refused to make eye contact.

"The win comes first," said Roselyn. "At any cost."

Undaunted, Ruby puffed out her chest. "Maybe *you* could have won the points if you hadn't been caught." It was only when a chill silence descended on the group that she realized she had said the wrong thing.

"He caught me too," said Akako.

"And me," said Voss.

Ruby dropped her gaze to the floor, feeling very alone.

All four girls leaped to attention as they heard a rapid *tump-tump-tump* approaching from the corridor outside.

When the door burst open a second later, they were standing in line, eyes dead ahead, expressions neutral.

"Rumours are spreading already." Marceline, their coach, limped in, surveying them sharply. "I'm here to give you the facts. Alarick's dead."

Ruby remained ramrod straight as Marceline approached her, leaning heavily on her cane. Their coach was an intimidating figure – tall and broad-shouldered, with a face so hard and a nose so straight it looked as if it could cut through sheet ice. The only part of her that didn't look as if it had been forged from steel was her right leg, which was several centimetres shorter than her left, and badly withered.

"You were there, Ruby," she said. "What happened?"

"I don't know," said Ruby. "It was so sudden."

"But he must have done something. Said something."

"Nothing," Ruby replied. "He just grabbed at his throat and fell over. I don't think he could breathe."

For a second, Ruby thought she saw her coach's lip tremble, but that was ridiculous. Marceline had hated Alarick more than anyone. Maybe she was going to cry tears of joy? But no. Marceline clenched her jaw and the moment passed.

"Hit the showers," she said. "The game's cancelled."

"But it's the final!" said Roselyn. "They can't!"

"They can and they have," said Marceline. "The judges have ruled no contest. Nobody wins."

"Can't we play someone else?" said Akako. "We've all worked so hard for this."

"Enough!" roared Marceline, her face turning as red as her team jersey. "I want all four of you washed and presentable in fifteen minutes. People are going to have lots of questions for you."

"Who?" asked Voss.

"The press," said Marceline. "Lawyers. The police. I don't know. But something went wrong and you girls were out there when it happened."

The team slouched to their lockers in nervous silence. Ruby knew what they were all thinking, because she was thinking it herself. *What had killed Alarick?* Close behind it was another, more worrying thought: Would people suspect her of playing a part in it?

Of course not, she told herself. *You didn't do anything.*

But what if someone else had?

She was so lost in thought that it took her three attempts at opening her locker before she remembered that the catch was broken, and the locker unusable. She'd had to borrow Marceline's instead. She made her way to it, pulled out her sports bag, and unzipped it.

She was surprised to find a glass bottle she didn't

recognize resting on the hooded top of her spare tracksuit. It was half-full with a bright yellow powder, and when she picked it up she saw a skull and crossbones stamped on the lid. The words LUPIX VENENUM were emblazoned on the label.

"What's this?" she wondered out loud.

The others were too preoccupied to notice. She shook the bottle and watched the powder swirl around inside. It was so fine that it flowed like dust.

She was still examining it, perplexed, when the locker room door burst open and four men charged in. They wore the teal uniforms and peaked caps of the Netherburg City Police Department, and their compact, gas-powered crossbows were raised.

Voss and Akako screamed, and Roselyn snatched up her sports bag, ready to swing it like a club.

"How dare you?" roared Marceline. "You can't be in here!" She advanced on the nearest officer, who fell back a step under her searing gaze.

"Yes, we can," said a voice that made the officers stand a little straighter. A large man strode into the room, dressed in a long coat and a baggy brown suit with a yellowed shirt. "Detective Breck, NCPD."

"I don't care who you are," said Marceline. "What are you doing here?"

Breck ran a hand over his greying crew cut and surveyed the room until his eyes fell on Ruby and the bottle. "Someone get that."

An officer hurried over, tore the bottle from Ruby's grasp and tossed it to Breck.

"Lupix Venenum," said Breck. "Just as I thought. Grab her."

"Hey!" Ruby struggled as two officers caught her by the wrists. "What are you doing?"

"Arresting you," said Breck. "For the murder of Alarick."

CHAPTER 3
Three Hours Earlier

"We're so proud of you, darling."

Ruby tried not to squirm as her mother licked a thumb and rubbed yet another imaginary blemish from Ruby's forehead. Her father, meanwhile, hovered beside her like a ghost, unsure of where to put himself.

"I'm fine, Mum. Please."

"We need you looking your best. Imagine what people would say if they saw you in the papers with a dirty face."

"It's Tooth and Claw, Mum. I'm going to be filthy by the end of the game."

Her mother licked her thumb again and scanned Ruby's face for another target. "All the more reason to have you spick and span now. Isn't that right, Harold?"

Ruby's dad clapped her on the shoulder. "Well done, sport."

Ruby took some comfort from the fact that she wasn't suffering alone. Voss was roughhousing with her older brothers, while Akako was lost in a scrum of aunts, uncles, cousins, and what appeared to be assorted friends and neighbours, all offering opinions on her hair, her posture, and whether red was really her colour. Even Roselyn's parents, stiff and elegant in their formal wear, were fussing with the cut of her tracksuit. Between them, the four families completely blocked the corridor outside the stadium's press room, and Ruby wondered whether the reporters inside could hear all of it. Maybe they were already writing it all down for this evening's papers.

"Where are my girls?"

With a huge sense of relief, Ruby saw Marceline cutting through the crowd like a ship through choppy waters. Everyone fell silent. Not even Akako's aunts wanted to get on the wrong side of Marceline.

"We're ready, Coach," said Roselyn, snapping to attention. Ruby, Akako and Voss followed suit.

"Good." Marceline surveyed the families with satisfaction. "Thank you all for trusting me with them. I promise to give them back in one piece." She allowed herself a tight little smile. "With the trophy."

The corridor erupted into cheers, and Ruby and her teammates exchanged excited looks. They were finally here – at the Tooth & Claw championship final.

For months, every minute of their lives outside school had been spent in the makeshift gym that Marceline had set up in a converted garage. Sprints, squats, push-ups, backflips, balance beams, standing jumps… It had been gruelling, but it forged them into a team and propelled them through the elimination rounds, the quarters and a nail-biter of a semi. Now the cup was within reach.

"We'll celebrate when we've won," said Marceline. "Right now, the team needs to meet the press. For the rest of you, there are ringside seats waiting upstairs, so go and enjoy yourselves."

Ruby hugged her mother, then drew her father into the embrace when he tried to pat her shoulder again. "Wish me luck." To her surprise, her mother's eyes sparkled with tears.

"Be safe out there, won't you?"

"I'll be fine, Mum."

"Oh, I know, but I worry about you being in the arena with…" She looked around and leaned in close. "…*you know who.*"

"You mean Alarick?"

"You've seen what he's capable of," said her mother,

shooting a meaningful look at Marceline's leg. "There's something of the wild animal about him."

Ruby gasped. "Mum, you can't say that about wolves any more!"

"And it's not true for most of them," her mother replied. "Goodness knows your father and I were delighted to help the Volkovs at number seventeen when they had their second litter of the year."

"Decent sorts," said Ruby's father. "Hard workers."

"But Alarick's different," said her mother. "There's too much of the Wild Wood in him."

Ruby was cringing so hard she felt she might turn inside out. "I won't let him lay a claw on me," she said. "I promise."

Her mother looked as if she had more to say, but Marceline appeared over her shoulder.

"Time's up, Mr and Mrs Calvino."

Ruby wondered if her mother would dare to argue. Luckily, her father intervened.

"Whatever happens, we're both over the moon for you all." He winked at Ruby as he and his wife followed the other families down the tunnel, their excited chatter fading into silence.

"Finally," sighed Marceline. "Ready?"

The team formed up, Roselyn in the lead. "Ready," she replied.

Marceline pushed the press-room door open with her cane. A wall of noise burst forth – strident voices, the pop of camera flashbulbs. "Then let's tell the world who we are."

"Marceline! Do you fancy your chances today?"

"Can you share any strategies with us?"

"How lucky do you feel to be here?"

Ruby squinted against the constant barrage of camera flashes. She and her teammates were perched on stools on a stage at the front of the room. A large circular microphone stood in front of them, the words WNBR – ON AIR burning in red neon around the rim. Beyond it, reporters and photographers filled every seat – or they would have, if they hadn't all been on their feet, shouting questions.

Marceline raised a hand for calm.

"Of course I fancy our chances," she said. "And we're not lucky at all – we've earned our place in this final. We outran six different wolves and outlasted every other human team. Even the Reichsburg Woodcutters, and they were the favourites at the start of the season."

"But now you're facing Alarick," shouted a male reporter from the back of the room. "He's been undefeated for a decade. Are you really the team to beat him?"

Marceline laughed. "What do you think, girls?" she asked, turning to the team. "Are we afraid of the big bad wolf?"

"No!" they cried together, eliciting a smattering of laughter from the reporters, and a fresh burst of flashes from the photographers.

"Charlotte Grimm, *Netherburg Gazette*," said a middle-aged woman in a matching red raincoat and trilby. "I want to ask Ruby how it feels to be the youngest human player ever to reach the final. Can a twelve-year-old really help win this game?"

Ruby grinned. "Watch me." There was another burst of camera flashes as Marceline placed a protective hand on her shoulder.

"Ruby's like me," said Marceline. "She grew up in the Narrows, which means she's been playing Tooth and Claw since she could walk. Trust me, she can handle this."

Pride swelled in Ruby until she felt she must be glowing with it.

Another reporter spoke up. "Wilhelm Jacobs, *Hillsborough Herald*. Is there any truth to the rumours that Ruby could replace Roselyn as team captain if today's game doesn't go your way?"

Ruby flinched. *What* rumours? Nevertheless, she couldn't help feeling a spark of excitement at the idea, and turned to Roselyn, only to find the older girl looking back at her with steel in her eyes.

Ruby was about to protest her innocence when the press-room doors slammed open.

"The game always goes *my* way," a low voice growled. "And there's nothing Ruby Calvino can do to stop it."

Everyone turned to look at Alarick, his massive frame filling the doorway. He posed, clearly relishing the attention, before leaping in one bound to the front of the stage. The cameras flashed like a lightning storm.

"What are you doing, you furry oaf?" said Marceline. "This is *our* press conference."

"Not any more," Alarick retorted. He snatched up the microphone and paraded back and forth across the stage, growling and gnashing his teeth at the press, who couldn't seem to get enough of him. Ruby realized that she and her teammates had already been sidelined.

"Alarick, are you going to make this your eleventh championship win in a row?"

"What's your secret, Alarick?"

"Is it true that you eat a whole raw pig for breakfast every day?"

Alarick just laughed, until Charlotte Grimm cut through the noise.

"Do you regret ending Marceline's career as a runner?"

A nervous hush descended, and all eyes turned to Marceline, whose mouth was now a thin hard line.

"She knew the risks of playing the game," Alarick replied. "If she didn't want to get caught, she should have run faster."

Ruby shot to her feet, furious. "It had nothing to do with risk," she said. "You fouled her!"

Alarick's maw split into a sharp-toothed smile. "What can I say? I'm a predator. Runners are just prey."

Roselyn rose from her stool to join Ruby. "Maybe *you* should be scared of *us*," she said. Voss and Akako sprang up, and together, the four girls linked arms.

Marceline put herself between them, standing toe to paw with Alarick. She was a head shorter than him, but held his gaze without blinking. "I'm going to get my revenge on the field," she said. "Just you wait."

Alarick bared his teeth. "Why, Grandma," he growled, "what big delusions you have."

"The nerve of him!" said Akako. "Crashing our big moment like that."

The press conference had become so heated that Marceline had dismissed the team to the sanctuary of the locker room, while she stayed behind to face down both

Alarick and the reporters. Ruby didn't envy her.

"He's trying to get into our heads," she said. "Throw us off our game."

"Maybe." Roselyn avoided looking at her and addressed the others instead. "Don't let him psych you out."

Voss leaned against her locker, looking haunted. "But it's true what he did to Marceline," she said. "She was a star player, and then…" She made a snapping motion with her hands. Ruby winced, and even Roselyn grimaced.

In the uneasiness that followed, it took Ruby just a minute to change out of her spare tracksuit and into the lightweight one she'd be wearing in the arena. It was the only outfit she owned that was designed to fit her exactly – light, breathable and bright red, which made it easy for her teammates to spot her during a match. The colouring was no use to Alarick though. Wolves were partially colour-blind, and saw much of the world in shades of grey. Their primary sense was smell. According to Marceline, a skilled wolf could smell you coming from fifteen metres away, and tell where you'd been several hours after you'd left.

Packing her spare tracksuit into her sports bag, Ruby crossed to the locker marked CALVINO. The key was in the lock, but when she turned it, the door remained firmly shut. She turned it the other way and tried again, without success.

"My locker's jammed," she complained to the room at large.

"Stick it in Marceline's," said Akako. "She won't mind."

Ruby crossed to the locker labelled COACH. It opened easily and she dumped her bag inside, on top of Marceline's.

"Warm-ups in ten minutes, everyone," said Roselyn, who was already stretching. "If you need to visit the little runner's room, go now."

Ruby felt the pre-game excitement building in her like a thunderstorm. It was the feeling you got just before unwrapping a birthday present – the fun of guessing what was coming, the ache of not quite knowing, the certainty of making sure you found out – but amplified a hundred times. It was scary and wonderful all at the same time.

But her excitement was derailed by a sudden, reckless idea. After Alarick's stunt in the press room, why shouldn't she strike back and try messing with *his* head? It might give them the edge they needed. "I'll be right back," she said, and slipped out into the busy corridor.

A minute later, she stood outside a door labelled HUNTER'S DEN. An overenthusiastic wolf – possibly Alarick himself

– had run their claws down it, leaving three deep gashes in the wood.

"Just get in his head," Ruby told herself. "Break his confidence."

"Whose head?" asked a voice at her ear. She yelped and rolled into a defensive crouch as her training kicked in.

A young wolf stood before her, watching in bemusement. He was about her own age, pudgy, with sleek chestnut fur and large orange eyes. He wore the garish green-and-purple uniform of the stadium staff, and the name tag pinned to his chest read FILLAN. He carried a yellow hatbox tied with a ribbon.

"Hello," said Fillan. "Are you supposed to be here?"

Ruby straightened and shot him a look, hoping that nobody had seen him catch her unawares. "Of course," she said. "I'm here for Alarick."

"Sorry," said Fillan, "but fans aren't permitted in the player areas. If you want an autograph, you'll have to wait in the stadium lobby after the game."

Ruby laughed, but he gestured up the corridor, inviting her to leave.

"Do I look like a fan?" she asked. "I'm Ruby Calvino."

"Who?"

"With the Netherburg Reds."

Fillan cocked his head to one side. "Is that the team playing in the final today?"

Ruby stared at him in astonishment. This was the biggest game of the year, and he didn't know who was playing? He had to be teasing her.

Before she could reply, however, the door opened and there stood Alarick.

"I thought I smelled company," he said. He squinted down his snout at Fillan. "You must be the cub they've assigned to look after me."

"This arrived for you," said Fillan, proffering the hatbox. "Flowers, I think."

"Splendid," said Alarick. "Bring them inside, please. And Ruby? To what do I owe the pleasure?"

She thrust out her chin. "You're going to lose today."

"I see," he replied. "You'd better come in as well." To her surprise, he ushered them both inside.

The den was stark and plain, with white-tiled floor and walls. After all, what was the point in colour when your clientele was colour-blind? Like all wolf spaces, however, it was filled with a cocktail of scents, dispersed by incense sticks around the room. Ruby detected the rich smells of moss and earth, and the colder, sharper tone of pine. There were other scents beyond her ability to make out, she knew.

A steel table stood in the centre of the room, piled high with raw pork chops. Alarick strolled over, picked one up and swallowed it in a few noisy bites. "Excuse me snacking," he said. "They're made from hand-reared pigs from the southern lowlands. Grain fed. Very expensive. I'd offer you some, but I've got nothing to cook them on."

Ruby scoffed. "Is this another intimidation tactic?"

"Not at all," Alarick replied. "Maybe Fillan would like one? They're very fresh."

Ruby couldn't be sure, but she thought she saw the young wolf's fur bristle for just a second.

"Not while I'm on duty," Fillan replied.

"Of course." Alarick licked his paws clean. "While you're here, could you replace these old incense sticks with my special ones, please? I had them custom made. I never prepare for a game without them."

"Sure." Fillan handed Alarick the hatbox, retrieved a dustpan and brush from a built-in cupboard in one wall, and set about sweeping the ash from the incense holders.

"Much appreciated," said Alarick. "Have you met Ruby, by the way? She's the best Tooth and Claw player of her generation." He chuckled. "Just don't tell her teammates. Roselyn strikes me as the jealous type."

Ruby was speechless. This wasn't the reception she

had expected at all. "This is some sort of trick," she said finally.

"Hardly." Alarick untied the ribbon on the hatbox and removed the lid. "Marceline wasn't joking when she said you're like her. She was the best too."

At the mention of her coach, Ruby mustered her anger, but her momentum was faltering. "Does that mean you're going to break my leg as well?"

Alarick winced. "Of course not," he said. "Besides, I'd have to catch you first, and that won't be easy. But I'm anxious to try."

"I…" she started. "Me too." *So much for getting under his skin*, she thought.

Alarick lifted a bouquet of yellow flowers from the hatbox. "Ah!" he said. "Wild Wood Roses. Someone knows my favourites." He buried his snout in them and inhaled, only to sneeze violently. "But they forgot to dust off the pollen," he said, wiping bright yellow powder from his nose.

"I'll light some extra citrus sticks for you," said Fillan, pulling a box of incense sticks from the cupboard. "They should help clear your nose in time for the game."

"Thank you," said Alarick. He sealed the flowers back in the box, but in so doing dislodged a small card, which fell from the bouquet's wrapping onto the floor. He snatched it up almost immediately, but not before Ruby saw the golden logo stamped on it – a rose surrounded by the outline of a house. Alarick flipped the card open and read whatever was inside. His ears wilted.

"What is it?" asked Ruby.

Alarick crushed the card in his fist. "Nothing," he said. He tossed the crumpled card over his shoulder, crossed to the door and opened it. "You should both go. The game starts soon."

Ruby glanced at Fillan, who looked equally surprised.

"I haven't finished the sticks yet," he said.

"I'll do it," said Alarick. "Just go, please."

They shuffled awkwardly past him into the corridor.

"If you need—" said Fillan, but the door slammed in their faces.

"That was weird, right?" said Ruby. "Who were those flowers from?"

"I have no idea," said Fillan. "They were waiting in the lobby. I just carried them down."

Ruby stared at the claw marks on the door. "Maybe it was a Reds fan sending him a rude message."

"That doesn't seem very nice."

She shrugged. "He's the big bad wolf. He'll get over it."

But as she hurried back to the locker room, she wondered how bad the message could have been. Alarick's reaction to it had been so strange. Was it fear? No, she wasn't convinced that Alarick even knew *how* to be afraid. Anger? Not even close. The question bothered her all the way to the locker room door, when it hit her all at once. Alarick, the most fearsome wolf in all of Netherburg, had looked defeated.

CHAPTER 4
Arresting Developments

Ruby struggled against the iron grip of the two police officers as they dragged her in front of Detective Breck.

"Let me go!" she shouted. "I didn't do anything!"

"Oh really?" Breck held up the bottle of Lupix Venenum, swirling the yellow powder inside it. "Then what's a nice girl like you doing with a deadly poison like this?"

"It's not mine," Ruby replied. "I found it in my bag, but I've never seen it before."

"Can you prove that?" When she didn't answer, he smirked. "Thought not."

He turned his back on her, only to find his path blocked by Marceline.

"Before you take another step, you can tell us why you're so sure Alarick was murdered."

"Because he shows all the signs of Lupix Venenum poisoning," Breck replied. "Muscle spasms, rigid jaw, foaming at the mouth. It's slow acting – takes at least an hour to kick in after being ingested or inhaled."

"It wasn't me!" said Ruby.

"We found a bunch of roses coated with this stuff in Alarick's room. It looks like pollen, and I'm betting he got a nose full of it, thanks to your girl here."

Marceline rapped her cane on the tiles. "Rubbish," she said. "If anyone should be a suspect, it's me. I was Alarick's biggest rival."

"Yeah, but you didn't sneak off to his den before the game," said Breck.

"Neither did Ruby," said Marceline.

Roselyn, Voss and Akako all nodded emphatically, but Ruby's stomach dropped through her feet.

"Actually, that's not quite true," she said.

There was a dreadful pause.

"Ruby?" said Marceline. "What did you do?"

"I wanted to mess with his head the way he tried to mess with ours," said Ruby. "But I had nothing to do with the flowers, I swear. I've never even heard of Lupix whatever before now."

Breck flexed his shoulders. "He threatened you at the press conference this morning, and you took it personally. You're in possession of the poison that killed him, and you were in his den at the same time as the flowers. You see the picture I'm painting here?" He motioned to his officers. "Take her in, boys."

The officers began manhandling Ruby towards the door.

"Wait!" said Ruby, struggling to free herself. "Please!"

Akako and Voss rushed at Ruby's captors and tried to prise their hands off her, until two more officers stepped in and pulled them away.

"I'll arrest all of you if I have to," said Breck.

Marceline slammed the tip of her cane down between his feet, with a crack as loud as a gunshot. "Do you honestly think a twelve-year-old girl killed the most famous wolf in Netherburg?"

Breck stared her down. "I think I've got enough evidence to take her in," he replied. "Want to join her?"

"Maybe I do," said Marceline.

With a humourless smile, he unclipped a set of handcuffs from his belt. "Fine by me."

"Stop!" cried Ruby. Panic swelled inside her, so hot and tight against her ribs that she struggled to breathe. But the thought of seeing Marceline subjected to the indignity of handcuffs was enough to make her swallow it. "Marceline, you can't help me like this."

A muscle in Marceline's jaw twitched. "I won't stand here and let them take you."

With a tremendous effort, Ruby forced herself to smile. "Then don't. Go and tell my parents what's happening and have them meet me at the police station. When the cops figure out I'm innocent, they'll have to let me go."

"That's 'if' not 'when', princess," said Breck. "And that's enough yammering. There's a nice cosy cell down at the precinct with your name on it."

Ruby held her head high and tried not to show how scared she was as the officers marched her out. She had expected to leave the stadium to cheering crowds, holding the Tooth & Claw Cup aloft. Instead, she was being marched out in shame, as a murder suspect.

CHAPTER 5
Fight or Flight

The police officers hustled Ruby through the winding maze of passages beneath the stadium. Her head was still spinning with the shock of it all – Alarick's death, the discovery of the poison in her bag, and now this. The shocked faces of stadium staff flashed by, and a shameful blush burned her cheeks as she imagined what they were all thinking: *Murderer!*

That was, until she saw a face she remembered.

"Fillan!" She dug her heels into the floor. "You were there. Tell them I didn't do it!"

All eyes turned to Fillan, who wilted like an old leaf as Breck signalled a halt. "What's this?" Breck demanded.

"That wolf boy," said Ruby. "He brought the flowers to Alarick's room. He can tell you I didn't touch them."

Breck hooked his thumbs into his belt. "That true, kid?"

Fillan flattened his ears against his head. "Yes, sir."

"Good." Breck turned to his men. "Arrest him too."

"What?" cried Ruby. "No! He's a witness, not a suspect!"

Fillan looked around in terror as two officers closed in on him. The other staff in the corridor all shrank back, as if he were suddenly contagious.

"He's an accomplice," said Breck. "You supplied the poison, he supplied the flowers. Case closed."

Ruby strained against the officers holding her arms. "But that's not true!" she said. "Don't you care what really happened?"

"I care about wrapping this up nice and quick," said Breck. "Human–wolf relations in this city are fractious enough as it is, and city hall wants to set an example."

A shiver of dread ran down Ruby's spine as the officers backed Fillan against the wall. She wasn't going to get any justice from these people; they would lock her up and forget about her because it was the easiest thing to do. And she had just dragged Fillan into it with her.

Before she quite knew what she was doing, she had jumped upward, raising her feet off the floor and letting the two officers gripping her arms take her weight. Caught off-balance, they toppled towards each other, their heads connecting with a dull *thunk*. Before they could react, she brought her heels down hard onto their toes. They screamed, their grips slackened, and she twisted free.

Breck grabbed for her, but she was used to outmanoeuvring wolves, and his effort was slow and clumsy in comparison. She dropped and rolled between his legs, popped up behind him, and delivered a quick backwards shove that was enough to send him stumbling into the two officers. All three men crashed to the ground in a heap.

"Stop her!" Breck yelled.

The officers closing in on Fillan whirled around, only to find that Ruby had already darted between them. She seized Fillan's hand.

"Run!"

She didn't wait for his response, but dragged him down the corridor and into a narrow side passage. There was a lot of cursing and stumbling behind them as Breck and his men regained their feet.

"What's happening?" Fillan wailed.

"We're escaping," she replied.

"But I haven't done anything wrong!" He tried to pull against her but she yanked him onward.

"Neither have I," she snapped. "But someone framed

me for Alarick's murder, and these idiots are going to lock us both up if we don't get away."

They turned into another corridor, dodging startled employees. The sound of pursuit was close behind them.

"Alarick was murdered?" said Fillan, horrified.

"Yes."

"By who?"

"I don't know!"

They reached a dead end and skidded to a halt.

"Now what?" asked Ruby, her panic rising.

The corridor was lined with doors and Fillan reached for the nearest. "In here," he said.

Breck led his officers at a breathless pace down the corridor until they hit the dead end.

"Start trying doors," he ordered. "They can't have gone far."

He watched with mounting frustration as the officers kicked in one door after another, bursting into cleaning cupboards, pipe rooms and storage spaces. They flushed out a few maintenance workers and a janitor, but there was no sign of the fugitives.

"They must have doubled back somehow," he said. "Let's go!"

They pushed back through the press of confused staff, and someone in a towering lumberjack costume, complete with an oversized head and huge rubber axe.

"What on earth is that?" asked Breck, trying to squeeze past.

"Team mascot, sir," one of his officers replied. "Reichsburg Woodcutters."

"Get it out of my way," Breck ordered. He shouldered his way past as the other officer opened an office door and practically shoved the mascot inside. "Call for backup. I want them found!"

The commotion of the search moved on. When the office was almost silent, Fillan's voice came from the mascot's mouth.

"D'you think they've gone?"

"How should I know?" Ruby replied from near the mascot's waist. "I can barely see a thing down here with your tail in my face."

"Sorry," said Fillan. There was an awkward pause as he moved it. "Did someone really murder Alarick?"

"Yes," she said. "The pollen on the flowers you brought him was actually poison." She realized she probably should have delivered the news more delicately when

Fillan flinched, almost toppling them both over.

"You mean I helped to kill him?" He let out a series of high, keening whimpers.

"Shh!" said Ruby. "None of this is your fault."

But Fillan was too panicked to listen. "I need to turn myself in," he said. "No wonder they want to arrest me! And now I've run away. That's a crime too!"

He was so agitated that Ruby had to dig her fingernails hard into his shins until he let out a yelp of pain.

"Listen," she said crossly. "You're not guilty and neither am I. But the police want someone to blame, and they're happy for us to take the fall. We *can't* hand ourselves in."

Fillan continued to whimper, although more quietly. "Then what do we do?"

"I don't know," said Ruby. "We need time to think. And somewhere safe, that doesn't stink of pickled onions."

"That's sweat," Fillan replied. "They never wash the mascot costumes between matches."

"Disgusting." She flexed her shoulders in an effort to spread Fillan's weight more evenly across them, but it wasn't easy. She was a runner, not a weightlifter, and her muscles were starting to cramp. "We need to get out of the stadium. Which way's the exit?"

"Turn left out of the door, straight ahead, second turn

on the right, then up the stairs," Fillan replied.

A button was missing from the lumberjack's plaid shirt, and by putting her eye to the hole, Ruby could just about see where they were going. With slow, aching steps, she manoeuvred the mascot forward. "Can you get the door?" she asked.

The costume had large cartoonish hands, with fingers like inflated sausages, so it took Fillan a few attempts to grasp the handle. He finally managed it, and they tottered out into the corridor.

"Straight ahead, second right?" Ruby whispered.

"And up the stairs," said Fillan.

"Let's go."

Ten agonizing minutes later, they emerged into the stadium's main concourse. It was a large, echoing space fashioned from red brick, with vaulted ceilings like an old church. A row of glass doors on its opposite side should have led to freedom, but the view outside was obscured by a crowd of humans and wolves, all banging on the glass. And between Ruby, Fillan and the exit was a second crowd, made up of stadium staff, security guards and police officers. Breck's reinforcements had arrived, and he stood at the heart of the chaos, barking orders.

"I want two teams covering the western entrance. Who's checking the fire escapes? And I don't care if we're already searching the basement level, search it again."

"Are you sure this is a good idea?" Fillan whispered.

Ruby wasn't sure at all, but before she could lie to him about it, a voice cut across the hubbub.

"You there! In the woodcutter mascot!"

Fillan dug his feet into Ruby's sides so sharply that she gasped – a rotund little man in a black suit and gleaming white spats was trotting towards them.

"Where have you been?" he asked. "We've got half the city outside, and they're going to riot if we don't stop them!"

Squinting through the hole in the costume, Ruby could just make out a name tag on the man's lapel: ADELMAR FLOSS, STADIUM MANAGER. When she realized that he was waiting for a response, she tapped Fillan's leg.

"Oh, um, right," said Fillan. "What do you want us – I mean, me – to do, sir?"

"To stand beside me as a show of support during my statement about Alarick, of course," said Floss. "The same as the others." He pointed to a small group of mascots huddled in front of the doors. There was Chanco, the wolf representing the Mountain Wolf Hunters' League; Oakley, the wise old tree of the Northtown Tree Fellers; and the nameless cherry tomato which served as the Reds' own mascot. In a previous life it had been a promotional gimmick for a struggling greengrocer, but its rictus grin and mad, staring eyes must have scared away more customers than it had attracted, because Marceline had snapped it up for a few florins when the business went under.

"Come on," snapped Floss, and set off towards the doors. Ruby lumbered after him, sweat rolling down her face. She wasn't sure how much longer she could keep going like this.

"Whatever happens, keep your eyes open for a chance to get away," she whispered.

They joined the other mascots, and Floss surveyed them all like a general inspecting his troops. "Remember, you're not just representing your teams out there but the sport of Tooth and Claw, so try to keep it upbeat." He paused. "But not *too* upbeat. Someone's died, after all." Then he called across the concourse. "Detective? We're ready."

To Ruby's horror, Breck strode over, accompanied by a phalanx of officers. They were all human, with the exception of two wolves, who stood upright in grey uniforms – Sniffers. Their noses were busy tasting the air, and they swung their heads from side to side, ears swivelling.

They're trying to find our scents, she thought. Her arms prickled with goosebumps.

Fillan must have guessed what she was thinking. "I don't think they can smell us through the stink," he whispered.

"Thank goodness for pickled onions." Nevertheless, Ruby's stomach knotted uncomfortably. It would take only one whiff to give them both away.

"Let's get this over with," said Breck. At his signal, the officers moved in a line to the doors, flung them open and began to push the crowd back. When they had cleared a space, he marched out after them. Floss trailed in his wake and motioned for the mascots to follow.

Steeling herself, Ruby manoeuvred herself and Fillan through the door and into the muted sunlight of Riding Hood Square.

Floss wasn't wrong – it really did look like a riot was brewing. Beyond the police line, the square was packed with people, both human and lupine, some of them carrying hastily made placards. JUSTICE FOR ALARICK, and WHO KILLED THE BIG BAD WOLF? There was a clear dividing line between the two groups, however, and they eyed each other with open hostility.

"This wasn't murder!" a man shouted. "And if it was, I bet another wolf did it!"

"Rubbish!" a female wolf replied. "I heard the Reds'

coach went crazy and chopped Alarick up into pieces, right there in the middle of the field."

A lectern and microphone were set in front of Floss, and the mascots spread out behind him. The little man cleared his throat.

"Ladies and gentlemen, humans and wolves," he began. "It is my sad duty to confirm the death of Alarick during today's cup final match. Ever since our city was founded, almost two centuries ago, the game of Tooth and Claw has brought humans and wolves together, and I'm sure you're all as shocked and saddened as I am to…"

As Floss spoke, Ruby peered out through the hole in their costume. Everyone in the square was focused on him, except for the police officers, who stood between him and the crowd, their backs to him. Very slowly, she began edging away from the lectern.

"What are you doing?" hissed Fillan.

"Trying to get us out of here."

"How?"

Ruby wished she knew. Maybe if she could get them into the crowd, the mass of bodies would provide some sort of cover? It wasn't much of a plan, but her legs were beginning to shake badly from the effort of carrying Fillan, and she knew she had to get out of the suit before she collapsed. But how to do that without drawing attention?

"...so without further ado, I'll hand over to Detective Breck." Floss wrapped up his eulogy and let Breck take his place at the lectern.

"Alarick's killers are on the run," said Breck, prompting gasps from the crowd. "Ruby Calvino of the Netherburg Reds, and a young wolf named Fillan Boreal." He gripped the lectern in his big hands. "Spread the word, keep your eyes open, and report any sightings immediately. Leave them nowhere to run to, nowhere to hide. Together, we can bring them to justice."

Fillan gave a piteous whine, and Ruby's stomach did a slow somersault. Breck was turning the whole city against them.

Abandoning subtlety, she charged forward and crashed into Oakley, the walking tree. The poor soul inside Oakley staggered forward, windmilling their arms, and crashed into Breck. With a crunch of splintered wood and fibreglass, Oakley, Breck and the lectern collapsed in a pile.

There was a moment of chaos, in which the line of officers turned to see what had happened. A few of them rushed to extract Breck from Oakley's branches, and Ruby seized her chance. She ran.

Or rather, she plodded at a brisk walking pace into the crowd, who were too interested in the commotion with

Oakley to pay them much attention. The sea of people parted slightly to let them through.

"Where are we going?" asked Fillan.

"Anywhere," she panted in response, a second before she tripped over someone's foot.

The costume didn't allow her to put her hands out to stop herself, so the lumberjack hit the pavement, shattering the papier-mâché head with a sickening crunch. Fillan cried out and rolled off her shoulders, pulling the costume in two.

Ruby sat up, swathed in the lumberjack's oversized jeans and boots, while Fillan emerged from the flannel shirt a few metres away.

People hurried to pull them both free of the wreckage.

"Are you okay?" asked a man in a Netherburg Reds top.

"I'm fine," said Ruby. She pulled the hood of her tracksuit up and turned away, but not before she saw the look of recognition in the fan's eyes.

"It's you!" He grabbed at her, so she kicked him hard in the shin, caught Fillan's hand, and shoved through the crowd towards the back of the square. But heads were already turning in their direction, and they quickly found themselves surrounded by a circle of stern faces and impassable bodies. Ruby looked around, desperate for some way out, but it was hopeless. They were trapped.

Then, from the direction of the stadium, she heard Breck's voice.

"After them!"

The line of police officers drew their nightsticks and surged into the crowd, swinging wildly. People fought to get clear, and it took only a few seconds for the panic to reach the people surrounding Ruby and Fillan. The wall of bodies quickly became a stampede.

"This way," said Ruby, and pulled Fillan with her as she joined the rush.

The stadium stood on Grau Kopf, a small island in the Fenris River, which split the city in two from north to south. Ruby and Fillan darted through the crowd towards Skoll Bridge, which linked the island to the east of the city.

"We can find somewhere to hide on the mainland," Ruby said.

They were halfway across the bridge when the headlong rush of people came to an abrupt halt. Another gang of police officers, some of them on horseback, had blockaded the far end.

"The other way!" said Ruby.

They turned, only to see Breck and his men closing in from the plaza. Breck was red-faced with anger, and his hair was studded with some of Oakley's paper leaves.

"It's over," he said. "Give yourselves up."

"We're innocent," said Fillan.

"Innocent people don't run," Breck replied.

The words struck Ruby like a blow. It was all so *unfair*. Breck didn't care if she was innocent or not – he just wanted a quick and easy win, and he was willing to destroy her whole future to get it.

Slowly, moving as one, the police on both ends of the bridge started to close in.

"You have the right to remain silent," said Breck, unclipping the handcuffs from his belt. "And frankly I don't care if you never say a word. We've got all the evidence we need."

Fillan started up a frightened whine deep in his throat. His ears were pressed flat against his head. "I can't go to prison," he said. "What would my parents say?"

Ruby looked from him to the cruel smile cut into the slab of Breck's face, and felt a sudden swell of determination. Someone had set her up, and now Fillan was about to pay the price alongside her. Whatever else happened, she couldn't allow that.

She gripped his paw tightly. "Take a deep breath," she said. "And whatever happens, don't let it out."

"Why?"

She turned to the parapet, put her head down and ran,

pulling him with her. "Because we're going to jump!"

They reached the edge of the bridge and she leaped, planting her leading foot on the parapet. The cold brown waters of the Fenris churned ten metres below them. *That's survivable*, she thought. *Right?*

"Stop!" yelled Breck.

She just had time to flash him a triumphant smile before she launched herself and Fillan over the edge. There was a sickening moment of free fall, the world spun around them, and then the Fenris rushed up to claim them.

CHAPTER 6
All Washed Up

For what felt like for ever, Ruby was aware of only two things: the burning in her lungs, as she fought to contain snatches of breath; and the tight grip of Fillan's paw in her hand. Everything else was a maelstrom of dark foamy water, propelling them both south through the city. She had no control over it, and no idea where it would take them.

So it was a shock when she collided with something rough and solid. The impact finally drove the air from her lungs, and she sucked down a mouthful of dirty water in its place. She panicked, choking and spluttering. This was it. She was going to drown.

At the same instant, she realized there was solid ground beneath her, and the water was finally shallow enough to allow her to stand. She did so, hacking up water. Her ponytail had come undone, so she wiped her soaking hair from her eyes and looked around.

She stood on a concrete boat ramp at the river's edge. Fillan was beside her on all fours, his fur bedraggled. Old cargo boats surrounded them, tended by a few men in sou'westers and grubby overalls. Nobody seemed the least bit interested in their arrival.

"Where are we?" Ruby wondered aloud.

"You almost killed me!" Fillan replied. "What if I couldn't swim?"

"We didn't have much choice," said Ruby. "Besides, everyone knows that wolves are strong swimmers."

"That's a lazy stereotype."

"Well, are you or not?"

Fillan pointedly looked away and shook himself dry, spraying water everywhere. "Fangbrook," he said, standing upright.

"What?"

He pointed. At the head of the boat ramp stood a huge building of iron and glass, like a gigantic greenhouse. The ramp led directly into the structure through a wrought-iron arch, which bore the words FANGBROOK MARKET.

Ruby looked around with new understanding. The

market building was surrounded by run-down warehouses and half-sunken jetties. They were in the docklands, in the southernmost reaches of the city. "Perfect," she said. "Let's get inside and come up with a strategy."

"A strategy for what?"

"For clearing our names, of course." She started up the ramp, only to realize that he wasn't following her. "What's wrong?"

He looked around nervously. "You must have heard about this place," he said. "They say it's run by criminals."

Ruby paused. Of course she'd heard of Fangbrook – it had a terrible reputation throughout the city. But right now it was their only option.

"We're wanted for murder," she replied. "We'll fit right in."

Fillan's tail wilted. Then, with obvious reluctance, he followed her up the ramp.

Fangbrook Market hall was like a grubby cathedral – huge iron ribs held up a roof of soiled glass panes that turned the afternoon sunlight as green as pond water. Its rows of stalls sold everything from fish to fur coats, and from incense sticks to jewellery of dubious origin. One stall even boasted enchanted acorns from the Talking Oaks in the depths of the Wild Wood, where untamed magic was said to linger.

"D'you think they're real?" asked Fillan as they passed.

"Don't be silly," said Ruby. "They're just normal acorns dipped in glitter."

They both kept their heads down, and Ruby noted that most of the other shoppers did likewise. Nobody here wanted to stand out.

"This might be a good place to lie low for a while," she said.

"I'm not so sure." Fillan pointed to a nearby stall, festooned with Tooth & Claw merchandise. There were team uniforms and plastic trophies, wolf masks and pennants. Most of the items were slightly off-colour, or had the team names misspelled, but hanging in a place of pride above it all was a big framed poster of the Netherburg Reds.

Ruby stared at herself, standing proud and defiant with her hands on her hips alongside her teammates. That had been her life just a few hours ago. Star player. Captain material. How had everything fallen apart so quickly?

It took her a moment to realize that the stallholder was staring back at her. She flinched, pulled her hood up and was about to hurry on when he called out.

"Ten florins for the top."

She paused. "What?"

The man was old and thin, with yellowing teeth and hair. "The tracksuit top," he said. "I'll give you ten for it."

She examined herself. The top was sodden, and almost brown with river filth. "Why do you want it?"

"Cos I been listenin' to the radio, and I knows who you is," he said. "And what you done."

"No you don't," she shot back. "Because I didn't do it."

The man shrugged. "Don't matter. It's still a collector's item."

Before Ruby could reply, she was interrupted by a low growl. "Was that you?" she asked Fillan.

"Of course not," he replied. "It's rude to growl in public."

She looked around, searching the aisle for any sign of threat. The growl came again.

"It's me!" she exclaimed, patting her stomach. "I think I'm starving."

Fillan turned to the stallholder. "Is there anywhere good to eat around here?"

"Plenty of places," the man replied. "If you got money."

Ruby fished in her empty pockets and sighed. "Ten florins, you said?"

"We'll take twenty for it," said Fillan.

The man looked unimpressed. "Twelve."

"Fifteen," said Fillan.

"Plus a change of clothes," added Ruby.

The man sucked his teeth. "Deal."

Ten minutes later, Ruby slipped between two stalls into a shadowy, litter-strewn space between a stall and the market's side wall. It was part storage area, part dumping ground, and a rat skittered out of her path as she joined Fillan on an overturned crate.

"Lunch," she said, handing him a package wrapped in greaseproof paper. She had exchanged her hoodie for a Woodcutters team jersey (spelled with one *t*, and slightly the wrong shade of blue) with a matching cap. Although it was only a disguise, she still felt a stab of guilt at wearing another team's uniform, and mouthed a silent prayer for forgiveness to Marceline and her teammates. Fillan, meanwhile, now wore a grey T-shirt with the legend MY PACK WENT TO NETHERBURG STADIUM AND ALL THEY GOT ME WAS THIS LOUSY T-SHIRT printed on the front.

Ruby unwrapped a package of her own to reveal a roast beef sandwich with all the trimmings. She took a huge bite, pausing to let the flavours run over her tongue. The warm burn of horseradish, the crunch of the lettuce, and the rich deep undertones of the beef mingled in her mouth.

She had never tasted anything so welcome.

"Do you really think we can clear our names?" asked Fillan. He unwrapped his lunch bundle, only to stare at the bloody lamb chop nestled inside it.

"I don't know," she said, spraying crumbs. "But someone out there caused all this, and we have to find them before the police find *us*."

"I've got a better idea," said Fillan. "Let's find a payphone and call our families. They can help us sort all this out."

At the thought of her parents, Ruby's appetite fled. What must they think of her now? They wouldn't really believe that she'd killed Alarick, would they?

"I don't think they can fix this," she said. "The police are going to keep blaming us unless we can find proof that somebody else killed Alarick."

Fillan's eyes widened. "You mean we're on our own?"

Ruby's spirits sank even lower. "Eat up. We'll need our strength."

But Fillan still didn't seem interested in his lamb chop. Ruby supposed he'd lost his appetite too.

As the silence dragged on, she finally turned to the question that had been building like a storm cloud in her mind ever since she'd found the poison.

"Who *did* kill Alarick?"

Fillan shook his head. "I have no idea."

She thought back to their meeting in the Hunter's Den, and frowned. "He seemed so…nice. It's almost like there were two different Alaricks – the horrible one who turned up to the press conference and the one we met. How do you explain it?"

"I can't," said Fillan. "I only met him when I brought him the flowers, and I was as surprised as you."

"That's another thing," said Ruby. "You were only joking about not knowing who I was, right?"

He looked taken aback. "Why would I be joking?"

"Because today was the biggest game of the season, and I'm the team's star player. If I do say so myself."

He shrugged. "I don't follow sports."

"You work at the stadium!"

"Only to pay for cooking classes."

Ruby blinked in surprise. "Since when do wolves cook?"

"I've always liked cooking," said Fillan. "I want to be a chef."

The laugh slipped out before Ruby could stop it, although she clapped her hand over her mouth.

"What's so funny?"

"Nothing," she said, blushing slightly. "Nothing at all."

His ears drooped. "You think we all eat our meat raw, don't you?"

"I never said that."

He sighed. "You didn't have to. I'm used to it."

An uncomfortable silence grew between them, until Ruby couldn't bear it.

"Alarick was eating *his* meat raw," she said.

"Alarick did lots of things that give wolves a bad image."

She scoffed. "He was the most popular wolf in the city."

"But for all the wrong reasons," said Fillan. "People only liked him because he scared them. They thought he was dangerous."

"He *was* dangerous."

"And that's not a good thing!" said Fillan. "Netherburg's always treated wolves differently, even though we've been here from the start. Alarick made that worse."

Ruby drew herself up. "Hey, buddy, you're talking to a Narrows girl here. I've never treated wolves differently."

"Really?" He raised an eyebrow. "Would you have laughed at the idea of a human wanting to cook?"

She opened her mouth to argue before realizing that no, of course she wouldn't have. The silence descended again, heavier than before.

Fillan sighed, wrapped up the lamb chop and set it aside. "We have to start thinking of some suspects. Who would want Alarick dead?"

"Only every runner who ever played against him," said Ruby.

"I'm serious. Someone out there must have really hated him."

The answer occurred to Ruby immediately, but she disliked the idea so intensely that she screwed her mouth shut.

"What's wrong?" asked Fillan.

"Nothing."

"You've thought of someone?" he asked.

"No." She scowled. "I mean, yes, but she didn't do it."

"Who?"

Ruby folded her arms, but Fillan continued to look at her, full of hope, until she cracked. "My coach, Marceline. She hated Alarick more than anyone."

"Great!"

"No, not great," she shot back. "Marceline's not a killer. She only wanted to see him lose the final."

Fillan rubbed his snout thoughtfully. "What if she was afraid he'd win?"

"Now you're just being rude."

"Sorry," he replied. "But it's a serious question. Maybe

Marceline wanted to make sure Alarick *couldn't* beat you."

Ruby shook her head. "I'm her protégé – the one who holds the team together. Even if she did kill Alarick, why would she frame me?"

Fillan's ears drooped. "Good question. Did you notice anything strange before the game? Anything out of place?"

They spent a moment buried in thought, until Ruby realized something.

"The locker," she said.

"What about it?"

"Mine was broken, so I used Marceline's."

"And?"

"And I dumped my bag inside, on top of hers."

Fillan sat up a bit straighter. "So if she hid the poison in her locker…"

"Or whoever else hid it there," she replied. "They might not have known it was my bag they were hiding it in. All our sports bags look the same. If the killer was in a hurry, they probably wouldn't have stopped to check what else was in there."

"So it *could* have been Marceline," said Fillan. "If she thought she was putting the poison back in her own bag after using it."

"I know she didn't do it," said Ruby. Still, a cold sense of dread closed around her like a fist. Was Marceline really capable of murder? Now that she had voiced the idea aloud, it seemed horribly plausible. "But yes. In theory. Perhaps."

She wasn't able to dwell on the thought, as the sounds of tramping boots and raised voices suddenly echoed through the market hall.

She and Fillan leaped to their feet.

"What's happening?" she said.

Fillan sniffed the air, and his hackles rose. "Police!"

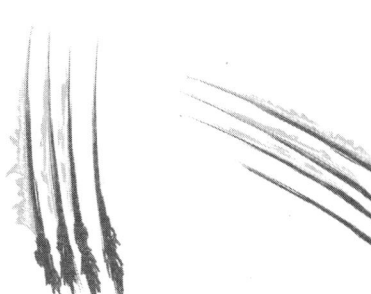

CHAPTER 7
Market Forces

Fangbrook Market echoed with the rattle of steel shutters, as stall owners promptly closed up shop and their clientele scattered.

"Block the exits!" came a booming voice. "Search everywhere!"

Ruby's throat tightened with fear. "That's Breck!"

She and Fillan crouched together in the gap between two stalls, watching the chaos unfold. She had no idea how the NCPD had tracked them here so quickly, but it was clearly time to leave, and fast. They stole into the aisle, only to find that a logjam of panicked shoppers had already formed at the nearest exit. People hammered on the doors in vain.

"We're trapped!" said Fillan.

Ruby's pulse quickened as visions of a cold, dark jail cell swam in her mind. "No," she said, pushing the thoughts aside. "Marceline always taught me that a hunter can't trap you unless you let them."

"What does that mean?"

She looked around, hoping against hope for a solution. She found one in a nearby fried chicken stall. It had a flat roof, and a wide metal chimney that ran up the market's side wall and out through an open glass roof pane. The opening was too small for an adult to fit through, but it looked just wide enough for her and Fillan.

"Can you climb?" she asked.

"I don't know."

"Time to find out."

As the crowd continued to bang on the doors, she gave Fillan a bunk-up onto the kiosk's roof. He reached down and helped her up.

"It's disgusting up here," he complained. He was right – the roof was coated in layers of dust and congealed grease, which squelched underfoot.

"Stop complaining and start climbing," she said.

The chimney was screwed into the brickwork with thick metal collars that made excellent handholds. It should have been easy to scale, but Ruby watched with mounting anxiety as Fillan hauled himself awkwardly up it, pausing every few seconds to look down.

"Hurry!" she hissed. Nobody had spotted them yet, but it was surely only a matter of time. If they were found now, it was over.

Fillan had almost made it to the top when Ruby heard Breck's voice directly behind her.

"Stop right there!"

Her heart leaped into her throat. Raising her hands, she turned around.

Breck and a handful of his officers stood together in front of the kiosk, their crossbows drawn. But, to her amazement, they weren't looking at her at all. Instead, they trained their weapons on a short, stocky man in a blue pinstriped suit with a yellow rose in his buttonhole, who swaggered towards them, chomping a cigar.

"Detective!" The man grinned, flashing a gold tooth. "Long time no see."

Ruby dropped flat and peered over the edge of the roof. Breck was so close, she could have reached down and tousled his hair.

"Jarvin," he snarled. "Out of the big house already?"

"Time off for good behaviour," the man replied.

"Yeah, you're a regular saint." Breck holstered his weapon and circled Jarvin, eyes narrowed in a flinty stare.

"The Oma Gang have got you running this dump again, I see."

Ruby caught her breath. She'd known that Fangbrook Market was crooked, but the Oma Gang were infamous.

"Those gangsters?" Jarvin feigned shock. "Detective, please, I manage this thrivin' community market that's full of legitimate businesses."

"Legitimate businesses that sell stolen goods and fake merchandise."

Jarvin's grin widened. "If you could pin any of that on me, you woulda done it already. So why don't you cut to the chase an' tell me why you're really here?"

Breck grunted. "We're looking for two fugitives. A human girl and a male wolf cub. You seen 'em?"

"I ain't seen nobody."

"Really." Breck held out a hand and one of his officers placed something in it – Ruby's filthy old Reds top. She suppressed a gasp at the sight of it.

"One of your legitimate businessmen saw 'em," said Breck. "Calvino and the cub are here, and if I find you're protecting them, there'll be hell to pay."

Jarvin calmly pulled a lighter from his pocket and lit his cigar. "If these kids turned up, I'd tell 'em the same thing I'm tellin' you." He took a long puff and blew a cloud of smoke in Breck's face. "Get lost."

Breck waved the smoke away and tossed the hoodie back to the officer. "Give that to the Sniffers and turn this market inside out." He gave Jarvin one last hard stare. "Make a nice big mess for our friend here."

Ruby lay in the grime, breathing hard, as Jarvin, Breck and the officers dispersed. Looking up, she saw that Fillan had vanished. That is, until he stuck his head in through the open glass roof pane.

Are you okay? he mouthed.

She nodded, wiped her greasy hands on her top and started climbing. She had spent hours shimmying up ropes and ladders in Marceline's basement gym, so the chimney posed no challenge at all. In no time, she emerged onto a narrow ledge at the base of the glass roof.

"We made it!" said Fillan.

"Barely." Despite her training, she was trembling.

After a few calming breaths, she peered into the alleyway two storeys below. Police officers hurried back and forth, reinforcing the blockades at the building's exits.

"Maybe we could hide up here until they leave," whispered Fillan.

She shook her head. "Sniffers are coming. We need to keep moving."

"But how?"

It was a good question. There was no way down from

the ledge, so she examined the warehouse across the alley – a dilapidated hulk of stained bricks, with rafters showing through its roof like old bones. It was too far to jump, but an arched iron sign marking the entrance to the docks connected the two buildings at the mouth of the alley.

"Follow me," she said.

They worked their way along the ledge to the front of the market until they overlooked a dingy street lined with old stores and workshops. Police wagons blocked the road, and throngs of officers hurried into the market.

"We can cross here," said Ruby, pointing along the sign to an empty window frame opposite.

"Impossible," said Fillan. "That sign's barely twenty centimetres wide."

"Just like a balance beam," she replied. "We use them in training all the time."

Fillan looked at her apprehensively. "You might, but I don't."

Ruby grunted impatiently. "It's not far, and if we're quick, nobody will see us."

"What if I fall?"

"Then they *will* see you, and you'll be badly hurt. So don't."

He started to protest, but she smiled at him and sprinted across the beam as easily as if she were running on solid ground. The blood pumped in her ears, and she felt the same thrill she had experienced in the arena. Someone was hunting her, but she was quick and she was cunning. Yes, it was scary, but it was also *fun*.

She vaulted through the window into a dusty storeroom piled high with boxes. No sounds of pursuit came from the street outside. She had made it.

Feeling rather smug, she waved to Fillan, who clearly wasn't having fun at all. His ears were flat against his head, and he stood, shivering, on the ledge.

"Quickly!" she said.

Wobbling slightly, Fillan set one foot on the beam. And froze.

"What's wrong?" said Ruby.

"I'm stuck!"

"On what?"

"On heights. I don't like heights."

Ruby's frustration ran headlong into a wave of guilt. Why should she expect Fillan to be as good at this as she was? Checking that they were still unobserved, she climbed back out of the window and crossed the sign again. "Keep your eyes on me," she said, taking his front paws in her hands.

Holding his gaze, she walked backwards as briskly as she dared. He wobbled a little, but kept pace with her until they reached the safety of the warehouse, where he finally dropped to all fours.

"I'm sorry," he said, trembling. "I slowed us down."

"But you did it." She patted his shoulder. "Well done."

He gave an embarrassed cough and stood upright. "We should go."

Ruby wanted to press him further but knew they were wasting time – Breck wasn't far behind them. "Agreed, but I'm not going anywhere without a plan."

"I thought we already had one," he replied. "Marceline. She's our only suspect."

"She's *not* a suspect!" Ruby stamped her foot. "I already told you that she's not a killer."

"Okay," said Fillan. "Let's go and ask her."

"What?"

"Let's find Marceline and ask her if she did it," said Fillan. "If she's innocent, you don't have to worry."

Ruby shook her head. "I already know she's innocent. And if she isn't, why would she tell us?"

"So you admit you're not sure."

Ruby glared at him, but her guts knotted as all her doubts flooded back. She hated the idea that Marceline might be guilty, but it had lodged in her mind now, and she couldn't prise it out. "She lives in the Oldgrove District," she said grudgingly.

"That's quite far," said Fillan.

"Then we'd better get started," she replied. "The sooner you hear the truth from her yourself, the sooner we can drop this."

CHAPTER 8
Suspicions

"Extra! Extra! Read all about it!"

A young newsboy stood atop an overturned crate at the corner of a busy intersection, spotlit by a street lamp as the sky darkened towards dusk. "Alarick's killers stalk the streets! Get all the latest in your evening *Gazette*!"

He waved a copy of the paper aloft and was quickly surrounded by a press of people, eager to buy copies.

Watching from across the street, Ruby was alarmed to see grainy photos of her and Fillan splashed across the front page. She pulled the hood of her Woodcutters jersey a little tighter and stuck to the shadowy fringes of the street.

She mostly went unnoticed. Ironically, most passers-by were too immersed in their newspapers, or conversations about Alarick's murder, to pay her any attention. Those who did glance her way saw only a lone girl in a blue top, her head down, walking calmly but purposefully north. Just another figure in the crowd.

Nevertheless, her heart felt as if it was climbing up her throat, and she flinched at every unexpected sound. Police cars cruised the streets, officers standing on the running boards and scanning the pavements.

"Stay vigilant," a voice barked through a bullhorn mounted to the roof of one car. "Report any suspicious individuals to the NCPD."

Whenever she saw them approaching, Ruby feigned interest in a shop window, or made sure she was out of sight behind someone else. All the cars had passed without stopping, but she knew her luck wouldn't hold for ever. She needed to get off the streets. She needed to get to Marceline's place.

But first she had to meet Fillan. It had been her idea to split up and make their way to Oldgrove separately. If the police were looking for the two of them together, she reasoned, they'd raise fewer suspicions travelling alone. He hadn't liked the idea, but she had insisted. Now, with a cold dread, she wondered if he had run into one of the patrols. The sick feeling only intensified as she reached their rendezvous point on the corner of Grove and Maple Streets. Fillan wasn't there.

It's fine, she told herself. *He just got held up.* But after ten minutes of fretful pacing outside a late-night laundromat, he still hadn't arrived. She wondered about going to look for him, but soon dismissed the idea – he could be anywhere, and what if they missed each other?

Another police car cruised through the junction and she quickly turned to the laundromat's window, only to come face to face with herself.

It was a wanted poster, printed in black and white but with stark red lettering. The laundromat attendant was pasting it onto the inside of the glass and, before she could look away, the two of them locked eyes. He smiled in greeting, then did a double take.

She didn't wait to see what his next reaction was, but hurried away onto Maple Street.

I'm sorry, Fillan, she thought as guilt welled up inside her. *I've got to keep moving.*

Marcclinc's apartment building was a modest brownstone halfway along Maple, with a short flight of steps leading up to a first-floor entrance. It was part of a row of identical buildings, indistinguishable from its neighbours apart from the police officer guarding the steps, and the crowd of press and onlookers on the pavement in front of it. Ruby recognized several of the reporters from that morning, including Charlotte Grimm and Wilhelm Jacobs.

She didn't dare stop, crossing by on the opposite side of the street. Of course the police and the press were going to be here! Why hadn't she realized that sooner? She cursed her lack of foresight and paused under a tree, close enough to watch the building but not so close that she would draw attention.

She needed a way in, and quickly. The front door clearly wasn't an option, so she'd need to be creative. Sideways thinking, Marceline called it.

Sideways...

The brownstones formed one long block that took up the whole side of the street. Residents in the neighbouring buildings had turned out onto the front steps to gawk at the crowd, and some of them had propped the front doors open.

Seeing her chance, Ruby pulled the peak of her cap low over her face and strolled as casually as she could to a building three doors down from Marceline's. None of the residents on the front steps paid her any attention as she climbed past them and entered the lobby.

"So far so good," she breathed. It was a relief just to be inside, even if the walls were cracked and stained with age. She took a moment to catch her breath. It felt as if the whole world was falling apart – first Alarick, then the poison and now Fillan – but Marceline would have answers. Solid, unshakable Marceline. Ruby grimaced at the prospect of confronting her about the murder, but she was impatient to banish the nagging doubt that Fillan had planted in her. Would Marceline be offended by the idea, or just laugh? Either way, once the question was dealt with, the two of them could start to build a *real* plan to fix things. Including finding Fillan.

Her determination restored, she climbed the building's winding central staircase, which took her from one narrow landing to another until she reached a fire door that led to the roof. As she had hoped, the roof stretched along the whole block of buildings, flat and uninterrupted. She ducked under washing lines and around chimneys until she reached the corresponding door into Marceline's building, where her quest ground to a sudden halt – there was no handle on the outside, and the door was shut fast.

She pushed at it, got her fingernails under the edge and tried to pull it, and finally thumped it in frustration. "Argh!" she said.

"Having trouble?" asked a voice.

Ruby whirled around. It was Fillan, his T-shirt stained and his fur matted. He looked exhausted, but he smiled.

"You're okay!" she said, throwing her arms around

him. She quickly recoiled, however, holding her nose. "Where have you been?"

"Hiding in a bin," he replied. "The police spotted me, so I took cover. They didn't find me, but they know I'm in the neighbourhood."

"And how did you find me up here?"

"I followed your scent, of course."

She held her breath and hugged him again. "I'm so glad to see you. And you were right, we shouldn't have split up."

"Can we stick together from now on?"

"Absolutely."

There was a screech of tyres from the street below. Cautiously, they approached the edge of the roof and peered over. Several police cars had drawn up and were disgorging officers, who spread out across the street, knocking on doors and shining flashlights into basement windows.

Ruby's skin prickled with fear as she and Fillan retreated to the door. "We can't go back down there," she said. "And we can't get into Marceline's from here. This door only opens one way."

Fillan looked troubled. "Can we get her to come and open it for us?"

"If we could speak to her from up here, we wouldn't need to get inside." Ruby started pacing again, trying to stop her fear from smothering her other thoughts. It was just a stupid door. All they needed was someone to open it…

The answer came to her a moment later, and she hurried to a row of nearby chimneys. She worked her way along them, sniffing. "Do any of these smell like menthol to you?"

Fillan cocked his head to one side. "Why?"

"Just smell them and tell me. My nose isn't as good as yours."

He joined her, his nose twitching. "This one," he said, pointing at the fifth chimney in the row.

"Brilliant." She leaned over the chimney and cleared her throat. "Hello? Mrs Deitz? We're here to talk to Marceline about the murder, but we're stuck on the roof."

"Who's Mrs Deitz?" said Fillan.

Ruby turned him away from the chimney and lowered her voice. "Marceline's neighbour, and the biggest gossip in Netherburg."

He stiffened. "Why did you tell her we're here?"

"Because she might let us in if she thinks we've got something scandalous to reveal."

"But we don't, do we?"

"Of course not, but she doesn't know that."

Fillan shifted nervously from foot to foot. "Won't she tell the police we're here?"

"Yes," said Ruby. "But hopefully not until she thinks she's got all the juicy details out of us. We just need to string her along for a bit."

Fillan stopped hopping and stared at her in horror. At the same moment, the fire door opened a crack, revealing a small, dark and deeply wrinkled face.

"Whatcha want?"

"Mrs Deitz!" Ruby turned to her with a smile. "Remember me? I train with Marceline."

Mrs Deitz adjusted her heavy glasses and looked both Ruby and Fillan over with surgical precision. Then she removed the foul-smelling menthol cigarette from the corner of her mouth, sucked at her gums and said, "You're that girl who's all over the news."

"That's all a *huge* misunderstanding," said Ruby. "I was with Alarick when he died, and we're here to talk it all out with Marceline. Is she home?"

Mrs Deitz pursed her lips, but there was no hiding the spark of interest in her eyes. "Yeah, she's home. I heard her movin' around just a minute ago. Not that I make a habit of listenin', you understand. Thin walls."

"Of course," said Ruby. "Can we come in? It's really important."

"And graphic," added Fillan.

The spark in Mrs Deitz's eyes grew into a hungry

flame. She pushed the door open, revealing her wizened frame clad in a purple nightgown and fluffy slippers. "Fine, but I'm keepin' my nose out of it. I like to mind my own business."

"Of course." Ruby sagged with relief. "We'll be out of your hair in no time."

They followed Mrs Deitz down two flights of stairs to the sixth floor. Sounds of laughter, music and muffled conversation emanated from behind the apartment doors they passed. People were at home, living their lives. Ruby envied them.

"How long do you think we can keep her interested?" whispered Fillan as they went.

"Long enough for us to speak with Marceline, I hope."

"And how long will that take?"

Ruby swallowed. "Not long."

At last they reached Marceline's door. Mrs Deitz watched greedily as Ruby gathered her courage and knocked. No answer came, but the door swung open under Ruby's hand.

"Marceline?" Ruby stepped inside. "It's me."

The apartment was small and spartan – little more than an open-plan kitchen with a sofa at one end, a bookcase, and a few old sporting trophies in a cabinet against one wall. The room lay in semi-darkness, lit only by the street lights from outside, and was clearly deserted.

"I definitely heard her in here," said Mrs Deitz, peering in from the landing.

Ruby grabbed Fillan and pulled him inside. "She probably just went out for some milk," she said. "Thanks for all your help, Mrs Deitz. We'll wait for her here."

Before Mrs Deitz could reply, Ruby shut the door and leaned against it.

"It worked!" said Fillan.

Ruby pressed a finger to her lips, then hooked a thumb at the door. *"She's listening,"* she mouthed. Sure enough, the shadows of Mrs Deitz's feet were visible in the light spilling under the door.

Ruby tiptoed to Fillan's side. "Where's Marceline?" she whispered.

Fillan's brow furrowed. "You said she just stepped outside."

"I lied. She'd never leave her door unlocked like that. She's too careful." She looked around the room again, all her doubts rushing back. "Something's wrong."

CHAPTER 9
Something Wicked

It didn't take long for Fangbrook Market to return to normal once the police left. After all, it wasn't the first raid that many of the stallholders had experienced, and there was still business to be done. The last constable was hardly out of the door before the sellers rolled up their shutters, set out their wares, and began barking for business once again.

Ned Grunge was less happy, however. Someone had clambered all over the roof of his fried chicken kiosk, and left a dent above his cooker hood.

"Bunch of hoodlums in this place," he muttered.

He wiped down the counter with a greasy rag. He never washed it, so it didn't so much clean up the grease as spread it more evenly. But that was how Ned liked it.

As his old man used to say, if it ain't greasy, it ain't food. That was the philosophy his father had lived by – although, admittedly, he hadn't lived very long – and it was a good business model. Grease, salt and free meat from the pigeon traps Ned set on the market roof each night. His little stall might not look like much, but it was one of the most profitable in Fangbrook.

He was reflecting on this when a shadow fell over him. He looked up, and jumped back so sharply that he crashed into the rotisserie. A figure wrapped in a rough grey cloak stood at the counter. They were so tall that only their torso was visible below the kiosk's roof, but they extended a large paw, clad in shaggy white fur. Its claws were long and black. A wolf.

Ned, who was never one to let primal terror get in the way of a sale, recovered himself. "What would you like, my lupine friend?" he asked. "I can do you some raw chicken. Two-for-one game day offer. Hey, it's terrible what happened to that Alarick, isn't it? Crying shame, if you ask me."

His customer growled – so deep that Ned felt it as a tremor in his bones.

"The girl and the cub. They were here." The voice was as cold and piercing as a winter wind, and Ned shivered involuntarily.

"Who?"

The wolf stooped. Most of his face was hidden inside the hood of his cloak, but his jaws protruded, and they looked big enough to take Ned's head off in one bite. A string of drool hung from them for a second and plopped onto the counter.

"Their scent leads here. To you." The wolf leaned into the kiosk, his snout pressing Ned against the back wall. "Talk."

"I don't know what you're talking about!"

The snout turned this way and that, sniffing the air. "Two hours ago."

"Two hours?" said Ned. "That was when the police shut the place down. I...I wasn't here then. Cops and me, we don't mix well, y'see." He was beginning to sweat with fear now.

A pause. Then, "I smell no lies on you, little man."

Ned laughed with relief. "Of course not. Honest as the day is long, me."

"Honest or not, they were here." The claws lashed out and seized Ned by the collar, lifting him off his feet.

"But, but, but...I don't know anything!"

"Not good enough." The wolf's jaws yawned open.

"The roof!" cried Ned. "Someone was on my roof!"

The jaws snapped shut a centimetre from his nose.

The claws released him and he dropped to the floor. By the time he had picked himself up again, the wolf was gone. There was an almighty crash on the roof, and the imprint of two great hind paws pushed through the thin metal. Then came a howl, long and low and chilling, that brought the whole market to a halt.

Ned rushed out of his kiosk, ready to sprint for his life. The wolf stood on top of it, staring up at the chimney and the open glass roof pane above it.

"What are you doing?" Ned cried.

The wolf turned to him. His eyes were twin pinpricks of baleful yellow, shining in the depths of the hood. "Hunting," he said.

With a ferocious leap, the wolf jumped straight up and smashed through one of the glass panes above.

Ned stood, dumbfounded, as the shards rained down on the crumpled roof of his kiosk.

"He didn't even buy any chicken," he grumbled.

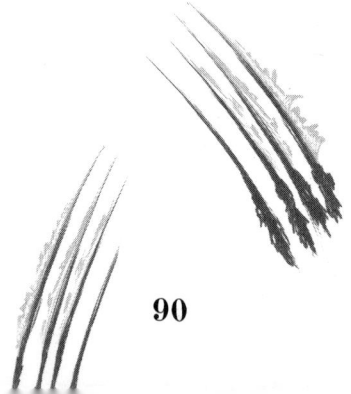

CHAPTER 10
Intruder Alert

Ruby peeped out through the blinds of Marceline's darkened apartment, being careful not to make herself too visible. The police officers were still patrolling the street, watched by the gaggle of reporters and onlookers. Behind her, the shadow of Mrs Deitz lingered outside the apartment door.

"I don't like this," Ruby murmured. "We need to figure out what's happened to Marceline before Mrs Deitz gets bored and starts blabbing that we're here."

"How do you know Marceline isn't visiting a neighbour?" whispered Fillan, who didn't seem to know where to put himself, so loitered awkwardly in the centre of the room.

"She doesn't get along with her neighbours. And

she never leaves her door unlocked, even when she's home."

"She can't have gone far," said Fillan. "Mrs Deitz said she heard her in here a few minutes ago."

Ruby pursed her lips. "She hasn't left the building through the front, or the press would be all over her. And she didn't pass us on our way down from the roof."

"So she's still in the building."

"Maybe." Ruby turned back to the window as she tried to unpick the puzzle. Why would Marceline leave her apartment but not the building? Had Mrs Deitz actually *seen* Marceline, or just heard someone moving around? She was about to voice the question when a sudden burst of static made her whirl around, heart pounding.

"Sorry!" Fillan grappled with the dial of a wireless radio on the kitchen counter. "I thought it might help mask our voices, so we don't have to whisper." The static gave way to a voice that almost made Ruby's heart stop beating altogether – her mother's.

"Darling, if you're listening to this, please, please, *please* get in touch."

"We only want to know that you're safe," added her father.

Ruby couldn't help but imagine him patting her on the shoulder as he spoke, and her breath hitched in her throat.

She left the window and joined Fillan, pressing her ear closer to the radio.

"If you're just joining us, this is Franz Rust for WNBR, bringing you the latest on the sensational hunt for the Tooth and Claw killers. A few hours ago, I spoke to Roselyn Brandt, team captain of the Netherburg Reds, who was with one of the suspects just moments before the terrible crime."

"Ruby and I don't always get along," came Roselyn's voice. "But I know she's innocent."

"How do you think this will impact her chances of succeeding you as team captain?" asked Rust.

The ensuing silence lasted so long that Ruby thought the radio might have died.

"No comment," said Roselyn at last.

Ruby grabbed the radio and switched it off. "We're wasting time."

"Hey, what about *my* parents?" said Fillan, forgetting to whisper. "What if they've got a message for me?" He reached for the radio but she swatted his hand away.

"We don't need messages, we need Marceline."

"Then where is she?"

"*I don't know!*" Ruby shouted, before clapping her hand over her mouth. Her heart thudded in her ears, and the apartment seemed small and airless all of a sudden.

She stumbled to the sofa, flopped onto it, and forced herself to breathe steadily. "We'll figure something out, but we can't stay here."

"We're running again?" Fillan's tail wilted. "I'm exhausted."

"Me too, but we can't fix this if we're in a jail cell."

He nodded wearily. "Can we at least use the bathroom first? I haven't been since..." He dropped his gaze to the floor. "Since we were in the river."

"Yuck!"

"Don't blame me," he replied. "That water was cold."

"Just hurry up," she said, unable to shake the feeling that she was missing something important. If it wasn't Marceline that Mrs Deitz had overheard in the apartment, then who was it? And what had they been doing here?

The thought was interrupted by Fillan, who had paused in the bathroom doorway.

"Can you smell something?" he asked.

"If it's the toilet, I don't want to know."

"No, it's..." He shut his eyes and sniffed. "Roses. Maybe Wild Wood Roses?"

She sat bolt upright. "Where? I don't see any."

"It's very faint, but it's coming from your direction."

She stood, and at the same instant a figure sprang up from behind the sofa. They were tall and human, but that was as much as she could make out. They wore black shapeless clothes, and their face was obscured by the hood of an oversized tracksuit top. Under one arm, they clutched a binder stuffed with papers.

"Who are you?" asked Ruby, alarmed.

The figure didn't speak, but vaulted over the sofa to land in front of them. They dropped into a crouch, ready to run. Ruby did likewise.

"Where's Marceline?" she said.

The figure darted left. Ruby moved to block them, only for the figure to break right instead. Ruby leaped after them, but the figure swung the binder at her face. It would have connected, had Fillan not thrown himself between them.

The blow struck him in the jaw, driving him back into Ruby. She tripped and fell, but not before she saw him sink his teeth into the intruder's hand.

With a cry of pain, it was all over; the figure shoved Fillan, who landed on Ruby, and leaped over them, abandoning the folder in a shower of papers. The figure threw the apartment door open, barged past a startled Mrs Deitz, and bolted out of sight along the landing.

"What's going on?" cried Mrs Deitz.

Ruby ignored her. "Fillan, are you hurt?"

He rolled off her and curled into a ball. "Oh no,"

he wailed. "Oh no, oh no, oh noooo!"

"What's wrong?" She scrambled to his side. There was blood on his snout.

"I bit them."

"Good."

He looked at her in horror. "But I'm a vegetarian!"

Ruby almost laughed with relief. Mrs Deitz, however, raised a trembling finger.

"You're a biter," she said. "A wild wolf!"

"I'm not wild," he protested.

"Help! Police!" Mrs Deitz's face was a mask of horror, but her eyes shone with barely suppressed glee. "The Tooth and Claw killers are here!"

Ruby dragged Fillan to his feet and bundled him to the door, almost tripping over the discarded binder in the process. She picked it up instinctively, along with a handful of the scattered papers; they might hold a clue about the mysterious intruder. "Out of our way," she said, elbowing Mrs Deitz aside.

The commotion had drawn several neighbours onto the landing, but they quickly backed away at the sight of Fillan's wide eyes and bloodied snout.

"Murderers!" Mrs Deitz cried. "They're here for Marceline Plats. Somebody stop them!"

CHAPTER 11
Surrounded

Ruby dropped into her runner's crouch, her eyes flicking around the landing. Marceline's neighbours stood in their doorways, looking nervously from her and the trembling form of Fillan beside her, to Mrs Deitz, who blocked the end of the landing, her eyes blazing.

Ruby made a quick assessment – Mrs Deitz couldn't hope to stop them herself, so was trying to goad the neighbours into doing it for her. But they were startled and uncertain, all waiting for someone else to make the first move. She and Fillan had to act before that happened.

"Run!" she yelled, and bolted for the stairs back to the roof. Fillan ran with her and, as they mounted the stairs to the seventh floor, they heard Mrs Deitz scream, "Don't all stand there! After them!"

There were a few seconds of confused muttering, then the sound of pursuing footsteps.

"Where are we going?" panted Fillan as they raced across the seventh-floor landing to the next flight of stairs.

"Up."

"Up where? Even if we get back into the other building, the police are all over the street."

"Well, we can't go down," she replied.

A door opened on the eighth-floor landing as they raced along it.

"What's all this racket?" said an old man in a vest and flat cap. He blinked at them with rheumy eyes.

Ruby stopped so suddenly that Fillan crashed into her.

Without further delay, she pulled him through the open doorway.

"Oi!" said the old man. "Whatcha doin'?"

Ruby pushed him inside, shut the door and leaned against it. "The Tooth and Claw killers are after us," she said. "We need somewhere to hide." The wood vibrated as their pursuers hurried past. When she heard them mount the final flight of stairs to the roof, she breathed a sigh of relief.

"The Tooth and Claw who?" said the old man. Fillan gave her an equally quizzical look. She winked at him.

"Killers," said Ruby. "They've been all over the news."

"I never listen to the news," said the man proudly. "Prefer to trust me own eyes and ears." He smacked his lips. "On the rampage, are they? Sounded like a lot of 'em out there."

"A horde," said Fillan, returning Ruby's wink. "They've got the building surrounded."

"And why are they after you?"

"Because, er...we're key witnesses," said Ruby. "They want to silence us before we can testify in court."

The man stroked his stubbly chin. "This city's gone to rack and ruin since we let the wolves have the vote. No offence."

Ruby and Fillan both grimaced but held their tongues.

"So you need a way out, eh?"

"Yes," said Ruby. "Can you help us?"

The man hawked back a load of phlegm, coughed and squinted at nothing. "Reckon I can," he said.

That was how, five minutes later, two figures climbed down the fire escape from the eighth floor into the alleyway behind the building. They were both small, their forms obscured by flat caps, flannel shirts and heavy twill trousers.

"I should probably feel guilty about lying to him like that," whispered Fillan as he and Ruby touched down onto the old cobbles. "But given his views on wolves, I think he owes me one."

The alley was deserted, although the sound of their pursuers filtered down from the rooftop overhead.

"Agreed," Ruby replied, securing the binder under her arm. "Now keep quiet and stay alert."

They emerged towards the far end of Maple Street. The police patrols had congregated outside Marceline's building and, as Ruby watched, a new squad barrelled in through the front door. Mrs Deitz stood on the front steps, gesticulating wildly as she related her tale to the assembled press.

"I bet she's loving that," said Ruby scornfully.

"They all think I'm a bite risk now," said Fillan, his voice hollow. "If they catch me, they'll muzzle me. Send me to the pound."

"I won't let them catch you," said Ruby. "And thanks. For taking the hit for me, I mean."

It was enough to briefly jolt him out of his malaise. "You're welcome."

They slipped around the corner and hurried away as more police cars screamed into the street behind them.

"Who would want to break into Marceline's apartment, anyway?" asked Fillan.

"I don't know," Ruby replied. "I thought we'd find some answers, but all we've got is more questions."

CHAPTER 12
Tactical Retreat

The sound of police sirens was audible as far away as Sawmill Drive, with its late-night delis and fleapit cinemas. The pavements were crowded, so Ruby and Fillan took shelter in a payphone booth before anyone could recognize them.

"We can't keep wandering the streets," she said. "We need a new plan."

"Agreed," he said. "Our last one got me punched in the mouth."

"It also got us this." She brandished the binder that the figure in black had dropped. "Whoever broke into Marceline's flat must have been stealing it when we interrupted them, which means it's important."

She opened the binder and they both leafed through

the papers inside. They were a jumble of official documents and handwritten notes – grocery receipts, Marceline's tenancy agreement, newspaper clippings of old Tooth & Claw games...

Then Ruby caught a glimpse of her own name. "What's this?" She pulled the sheet free and angled it into the neon-pink light of a nearby cinema awning. "Team assessments. She's been rating our performances." She began reading hungrily, only for Fillan to slap his hand down over the sheet.

"Focus. That's not what we're looking for."

She knew he was right, but couldn't escape a nagging question – *What if Marceline really does plan to make me team captain?*

"Here." She tore the assessments free and thrust the binder at Fillan. "I'll read these, you check the rest."

Ignoring his sigh, she scanned the entries. They were mostly records of past game scores, dating back several months, with notes of who had claimed which points. A contented glow blossomed in her as she tallied up her total – she was easily the highest scoring member of the team.

Next came Marceline's appraisals, written in cramped handwriting beneath each player's name. She read quickly through Roselyn's, Voss's and Akako's, but they were surprisingly dry and technical. They ran onto the next page, so she took a deep breath and turned it over.

There was only one sentence written under her own name. It was dated just a few weeks earlier and stood out in heavy capital letters: *SHE NEEDS TO FAIL.*

Ruby's excitement vanished in a rush, leaving a cold, leaden sensation in its wake. Her shock must have been obvious, because Fillan looked up from the binder.

"Is something wrong?"

She folded up the sheet and slipped it into her pocket. "Nothing." She was worried he might not believe her, but he shrugged and prodded the open binder.

"Good, because I've found something."

He unfastened a document and passed it to her. It was printed on heavy, official-looking paper and marked *Transfer of Deeds.*

"What does this mean?" she asked.

"A deed is proof of ownership of a property," said Fillan. "Somebody owned a building and they gave it to Marceline."

Ruby frowned. "Marceline doesn't own property. She can barely afford the rent on her apartment." She read down the page until she found the property's address. "The Peterson Paper Mill!"

"You know it?"

"It's in the Narrows, not far from my house. But it's been abandoned for years."

"That's not the strangest thing about it." Fillan pointed to a pair of signatures at the bottom of the page. "This certifies the transfer of the paper mill to Marceline Plats... from Alarick."

They locked eyes.

"That's impossible," Ruby said.

"It's here in black and white," he replied. "But why would Alarick own an abandoned paper mill? And why give it to Marceline if they hated each other?"

Ruby shook her head, too stunned to reply. This had to be wrong. Marceline would never strike any sort of deal with Alarick.

"She never mentioned it to you?" asked Fillan.

"Never." The word came out as a whisper – all the air was gone from her lungs, and she braced herself against the inside of the booth as her head swam. What did all this mean? Ruby had spent the last year moulding herself in her coach's image, trying to think like her, to act like her. To be the best, like her. All to beat Alarick and get Marceline the justice she deserved. Now Ruby wasn't even sure who Marceline was.

SHE NEEDS TO FAIL.

"Are you sure you're okay?" asked Fillan, closing the binder.

Ruby shut her eyes, took a deep, deep breath, and opened them again. "The new plan's the same as the old plan," she said. "We find Marceline."

Fillan looked sceptical. "She could be anywhere."

"We'll start at the Peterson Paper Mill. It's hers, after all. And it connects her to Alarick."

Fillan took the deed back, folded it up carefully and tucked it into his T-shirt. "It's certainly suspicious. Do you think the person we caught in Marceline's flat was after the deeds?"

"They were hardly after the shopping lists," said Ruby.

"Which means that somebody else out there knows about this."

His words twisted like a knife in Ruby's heart. It hurt to imagine that a stranger knew more about Marceline's life than she did.

"You said the intruder smelled like Wild Wood Roses," she said. "Do you think they poisoned Alarick?"

"It's possible," said Fillan.

"Alarick said they were his favourites…" Ruby cast her mind back to their meeting in the Hunter's Den. "If only I'd got a look at that note that came with them. He seemed so upset by it."

"Oh!" Fillan's ears perked up. "I totally forgot. I read it."

"What? When?"

"During the game. They sent me back to the Hunter's Den to tidy up and get it ready for Alarick, post-match. The note was still lying on the floor where he'd tossed it." He gave her a proud smile.

"Well?"

"It said, 'Pay your dues'."

The hairs on Ruby's arms bristled as the memory of her encounter with Alarick in the arena resurfaced. "That's what he said to me, right before he died. That it was time to pay his dues."

Fillan's ears twitched. "What do you think he meant?"

Ruby shook her head. "I don't know, but he obviously understood the message on the card. Maybe it was a warning."

Fillan drummed his claws on the binder. "You think he knew he was going to die?"

Ruby reflected for a moment. "No, he was too shocked when it happened. But there's some connection we're not seeing."

She hated this not knowing. It felt wrong, as if part of the world no longer fitted, and nothing could be normal until it was fixed. But she had no idea how to fix it. "Was the note signed?" she asked.

"No. There was just that logo on it. The rose inside the house."

The wail of a siren cut through the noise of the street, and they huddled together as a police car cruised past.

"Time to move," said Ruby.

Fillan sighed. "I suppose so."

"Don't worry," she said. "Marceline will have the answers." What she didn't add was that she was no longer so sure that she wanted to hear them.

From a rooftop across the street, the cloaked figure of the white wolf watched intently. He had tracked his prey here from the market, through the city's conflicting scents and sounds. He hated this place, with its brick and concrete, and buzzing electric lights. He longed for the soft darkness of the Wild Wood, where the hunt was always simpler. Purer. Why did humans insist on making the world so complicated?

But no matter. He watched as the girl and the wolf cub broke cover and crossed the street, disappearing into an alley. He kept pace with them as they ran, jumping easily from rooftop to rooftop.

He smiled in the shadows of his hood. He was ready to strike at the opportune moment, and his quarry didn't even know he was coming. The hunt would soon be over.

CHAPTER 13
Home Turf

The Narrows lay in the eastern part of the city, separated from Oldgrove by an industrial canal. Its streets were narrow, twisting and quiet, and as soon as she stepped into them, a melancholy ache settled in Ruby's chest.

"I'm almost home," she said. "Mum and Dad are just a few streets away."

"We could check in on them," said Fillan.

The ache deepened, and she paused in the lee of an overhanging building. It would be so easy, wouldn't it? She could at least see the house, maybe peer in through the front window and catch just a glimpse of them. Her mum would be cleaning, as she always did when she was stressed. Her dad would be putting on a brave face, but he wouldn't be able to stop himself pacing around the living room…

She forced the image from her mind. "No. The police will probably be watching my house, and we can't afford the time anyway. There's no going home until this is over."

His tail drooped. "I just want to let my parents know I'm all right."

"I know." She put a reassuring hand on his shoulder. "Where do you live, anyway?"

"West of the river."

She arched an eyebrow. "The swanky side of town?"

"Hey, it's not all swanky. The really posh neighbourhoods still don't let wolves move in."

She looked at him sharply. "But that's illegal!"

"Of course, but it still happens. Apartments are suddenly unavailable, or the price doubles when it's a wolf asking."

"I had no idea. I'm so sorry."

He shrugged, but she guessed that he wasn't as uninterested as he looked.

"Let's get this done so we can both go home," he said.

They struck off down one of the side streets, keeping to the shadows. As they went, Fillan took in the empty shop units, the pitted cobblestones and the dilapidated half-timbered houses.

"Why does everything look so...old?"

"Because it is," Ruby replied. "The Narrows started as a logging outpost for the first human pioneers. It's where Netherburg was born. And it's where Tooth and Claw started, of course. That's why the Narrows still turns out the best players."

"Including you?"

"Me, Marceline, Alarick. We all learned it on the streets."

They paused at a junction, and she pointed at a couple of ragged flags dangling from a shop sign overhead. "Ten points for the Mill Street Machines. I played with them when I was younger."

Fillan surveyed the street signs. "If this is Mill Street then we must be close."

Sure enough, they soon found themselves in a dilapidated square, with a venerable oak standing in the centre. Rising behind a tall metal fence beyond it was the Peterson Paper Mill. Its arched windows were dirty and broken, and its chimney towered like a spire over the surrounding streets.

"What would Alarick *or* Marceline want with this place?" said Fillan.

"I have no idea. It's been empty for as long as I can remember." She pointed to a peeling red sign attached to the fence. DANGER. UNSAFE STRUCTURE.

"Do you really think we'll find any answers inside?"

Ruby brushed the sheet of player assessments in her pocket. "We definitely won't find any standing out here."

The mill's gates were padlocked, but the fence was so old and twisted that it was easy for them to squeeze through. They crossed the empty lumber yard to the building's entrance. Ruby had her hand on the door when Fillan grabbed her shoulder.

"Look!" he hissed.

She followed his pointing finger back across the square. "I don't see anything," she whispered.

"Someone was there."

She squinted into the gloom. "The police?"

"I don't think so. They were tall, and really pale. A wolf, I think."

"There are plenty of wolves around here," she replied.

They both stood and watched in silence. When nothing happened, Ruby lifted the heavy latch on the mill doors, which yawned open with a groan. "Let's see what's in here."

The interior of the mill was almost as big as the Fangbrook Market hall, but instead of noise and bustle, it was a place of deathly silence. The hulks of old machines rotted around them, water dripped from holes in the ceiling high above, and shafts of moonlight cast eerie spotlights on the ground.

Ruby's determination faltered. "Can you smell anything?"

"With all the rot and engine oil in here, I'm amazed I can smell at all," Fillan replied.

She hugged herself against the cold. "Let's look around."

They explored the mill floor, sweeping it from one end to the other until it was clear that the building was exactly what it looked like – an empty ruin.

Ruby sat down heavily on a broken conveyor belt. "So much for answers," she sighed. "There's nothing special about this building at all."

"There must be," said Fillan, joining her. "Alarick wouldn't have given it to Marceline otherwise."

"Maybe you're wrong about that document." Ruby gestured at the broken machines. "Why would anyone want this place?"

His ears wilted with disappointment, but immediately perked up again. "Wait, do you hear that?"

Through the gloom, Ruby heard a distant door swing shut, followed by a sound that made the hairs on her arms stand up – the *tump-tump-tump* of a steel-tipped cane against concrete.

Marceline loomed out of the darkness like a ghost. Her face was pale and drawn, but her expression was determined. "Ruby!" She stopped short. "You're safe!"

Part of Ruby was so relieved to finally see Marceline that she had to fight the urge to run and embrace her. But the fact that her coach was here proved Fillan right – she really did have a connection with the building, and with Alarick. Was it a connection that had led to murder? Ruby didn't have the courage to ask that question yet, so she simply said, "You weren't at your apartment."

"I've been at the police station all afternoon, arguing with idiots," said Marceline. "I didn't have the strength to face the press at my apartment, so I came here to clear my head."

"Why here?" asked Fillan.

The question must have struck a nerve, as a look of annoyance flashed across Marceline's face. "I have my reasons." She started towards them, but they both scrambled to their feet and retreated. "What's wrong?"

With mounting dread, Ruby realized she couldn't avoid the question any longer. She balled her fists and said, "Did you kill Alarick?"

Marceline snorted. "Don't be ridiculous."

"Answer the question."

"Of course I didn't."

Ruby scrutinized Marceline's face for any hint of deceit. "I want to believe you."

"Then do. I've never lied to you before."

"Really?" Ruby pulled the player assessment from her pocket. "This says you wanted me to fail, and today I did. I would have scored the winning points if Alarick hadn't died. Did you know it was going to happen?"

Marceline's expression hardened. "How did you get that?"

Fillan, who had been watching Ruby in surprise, pulled the deed from inside his T-shirt. "We also know that Alarick bought this building for you."

"So don't pretend you haven't been hiding things," said Ruby. "What was really going on with you and Alarick?"

Marceline looked from Ruby to Fillan. "Alarick was my rival." She gave a long, heavy sigh. "But he was also my best friend."

CHAPTER 14
Broken Future

Marceline's words were so unexpected that Ruby needed a few seconds to be sure she understood them. "He was *what*?"

"My best friend," said Marceline. "The closest I've ever had."

Ruby gawped at her in disbelief. "But...but how?"

Marceline gestured to the broken conveyor belt and the three of them sat down together, in the shadow of one of the great paper rolling machines. The mill echoed with the steady drip of water into stagnant puddles as Marceline spoke.

"I've known Alarick since I was very young. I was raised in a tenement – three families in a single room. Outside toilet. No electricity. So I did what kids in the

Narrows always do, and spent my days on the streets playing Tooth and Claw. Pick-up games, scrimmages. Just kids filling time. Alarick was always around. He lived on the streets, and he'd play for scraps of food. Whenever he won, he got fed."

"So he learned to win quickly," said Ruby.

"Exactly," Marceline replied. "The better he got, the better I had to be if I wanted to stand a chance of beating him. We spent every day together, testing each other to the limit. We loved it." She smiled sadly. "When we hit our teens, we were talent spotted and moved into the professional game together. I became the Reds' star player, and Alarick, well…"

She lapsed into silence.

"What happened?" asked Fillan.

"Alarick was smart. He realized that the fans didn't just want an opponent, they wanted a villain. So that's what he gave them. He leaned into all the old stereotypes from our histories – the ravenous beast, waiting to pounce on plucky young heroines."

Fillan scowled. "The big bad wolf."

"It was just a bit of theatre," said Marceline. "But it worked. People loved to hate him."

Ruby again recalled the difference between Alarick's behaviour at the press conference and the Hunter's Den.

"You can't expect me to believe his whole personality was an act," she said.

Marceline laced her fingers over the head of her cane and rested her chin on them. "It was an act when he started. But as time passed and he got more successful, he made a stupid mistake – he started to believe his own hype. In his eyes, he really was an apex predator, and it made him conceited. He started to play dirty – just bending the rules at first, but then bigger infractions and deliberate fouls. He even started bullying players on and off the field. People were scared to face him, which only enhanced his reputation. We drifted apart, but I didn't realize how badly until one match, when I was about to slip past him and score the winning points..."

Fillan winced. "Your leg."

Marceline patted herself on the thigh. "He didn't seem to care that he'd done it, and that hurt most of all." She gazed up at the patches of sky visible through the roof. "Arrogance can turn even the best player into a liability. Including you, Ruby."

Ruby started. "What do you mean?"

"You're the best player on the team, but the trouble is you know it. You *expect* to win, and you're starting to see your teammates as a hindrance."

Ruby flushed. "That's not true!"

"Isn't it?" Marceline's expression was one of cold professionalism. "Do you believe that anyone but you could have beaten Alarick today?"

Ruby flinched. Of course she didn't believe that, but she hadn't realized it until now. "We all contributed," she said hurriedly. "Every point counts."

"But you never doubted that you'd score the winning ones," said Marceline. "That's the problem. You treat your teammates like a support act, while you're the main attraction."

Ruby's embarrassment flared into anger. "It's not my fault they all got caught. I *had* to score the winning points because I was the only player left."

"And Alarick might have caught you too if he hadn't…" Marceline's voice cracked and she cut herself short. "My point, Ruby, is that you're not immune to failure, and the sooner you realize that, the less of a shock it'll be when you really mess up."

Ruby's anger was approaching blast-furnace levels. Beads of sweat stood out on her forehead. "It sounds like you *wanted* Alarick to catch me!"

"After I spent ten years trying to build a team that could take him down?" Marceline snorted. "Don't be ridiculous."

Ruby retreated into sullen silence. She'd never

received such criticism from Marceline before, and it stung bitterly.

Beside her, Fillan cleared his throat a little awkwardly. "You still haven't explained what the paper mill's got to do with all this," he said.

Marceline brightened. "It's Alarick's apology to me," she said. "It's the future."

He gave her a puzzled look. "Of what?"

"Of Tooth and Claw." Marceline levered herself to her feet and turned to face them, like a teacher addressing her students. "It doesn't look like much now, but this building is going to change every—"

A ragged shape burst out of the darkness and slammed into her side, sending her flying. Ruby was on her feet in an instant, but the shape swiped at her with a long, furry white arm. She somersaulted backwards, landing on the conveyor belt.

The shape reared up. It was a wolf in a long, hooded cloak. Its white paws and snout glowed eerily in the shafts of moonlight piercing the roof.

"Who are you?" said Ruby, trying to keep the fear from her voice.

"The hunter." The voice that issued from the hood made the hairs on Ruby's arms prickle. "And you are the prey."

"This must be a mistake," said Fillan, taking Ruby's hand and slowly backing away along the conveyor belt. "We're not here to play Tooth and Claw."

"No games," said the wolf. "A *real* hunt."

He cast his cloak aside, and Ruby gasped. He was unlike any wolf she had ever seen. His fur was snow white, and his frame was lanky but solid with muscle, like lengths of knotted rope clad in fur.

"I am Hardulph," the wolf said. "I have fought the talking bears of the north mountains, stalked the gingerbread witch of the Usbrid Woods, and now" – he bared his long, wicked teeth – "I have been sent for the wolf killers." Then he charged.

CHAPTER 15
What Big Teeth You Have

Ruby shoved Fillan off the conveyor belt as Hardulph barrelled towards them. Fillan rolled clear but she was left staring into Hardulph's gaping maw. It would have snapped shut on her head if Marceline hadn't reappeared with a cry and slammed her cane into the wolf's side. Instead, his teeth grazed Ruby's shoulder, tearing through her top and drawing blood.

Ruby screamed, and Hardulph rounded on Marceline. "I'm not here for you," he growled.

Marceline circled him, limping badly. "Tough." She seized Ruby's hood and dragged her to Fillan's side. "You two get out of here. I'll keep him busy."

Pain blazed in Ruby's shoulder, and blood seeped between her fingers as she pressed a hand to it. Ruby's head spun. A real hunt, against a wild wolf? Impossible.

There was more of her blood around Hardulph's jaws and she watched, disgusted, as his tongue snaked out and lapped his fur clean.

"Delicious," he growled.

"You heard Marceline," said Fillan, tugging at Ruby's sleeve. "Let's go."

She pulled back. "I'm not leaving."

"Stop arguing and scram," said Marceline.

Hardulph feinted left, but Ruby's coach was ready for him and brought her cane up like a club when he tried to dart right. He growled, his eyes flashing red in the half-light. Marceline backed away from him, shepherding Ruby and Fillan with her.

"I'm sick of running," said Ruby. "I'm going to stay and fight until I get some answers."

"You want answers?" said Marceline. "Find Charlotte Grimm."

"The reporter?" said Ruby.

"She can tell you about this place. She knows the plan."

"What plan?" asked Ruby.

If Marceline answered, her words were smothered by a low growl from Hardulph. He lunged, and caught Marceline's cane in his paw when she swung it at him.

With a powerful twist, he pulled it from her grasp and she toppled to the floor.

"That's better." He stepped over her and tossed the cane aside. Then, with a satisfied leer, he sprang, only for his jaws to snap shut a centimetre from Ruby's nose. He turned and snarled – Marceline had caught his tail with both hands.

"I trained you to run," she said to Ruby through clenched teeth. "So *run!*"

The last thing Ruby saw before she and Fillan burst outside into the lumber yard was Hardulph falling on Marceline in a whirl of furious teeth and claws.

CHAPTER 16
A Rubbish Escape

Ruby and Fillan ran until their lungs burned, down backstreets and passageways, through courtyards and over fences, until they collapsed on the towpath of the old canal. The bright lights of the city shone out across the water, but Ruby couldn't find any comfort in them. She was breathless and terrified, still clutching the deep scratch on her shoulder.

"Here." Fillan wriggled out of his T-shirt and tore it into strips. "I learned this at Junior Wolf Scouts." He tied the strips tightly under Ruby's arm and over her shoulder. The stinging pressure made her eyes water, but the trickle of blood stopped.

"Marceline," she said. "We have to go back for her."

"We can't."

"But she could be hurt!"

He shook his head. "She gave us a chance to escape. If we go back now, she'll have risked her life for nothing."

Anger bubbled up in Ruby, so hot and acidic that she felt she might choke on it. But underneath it was an even worse feeling – shame. Marceline had given everything to help them, even after Ruby had suspected the worst of her.

She jumped as a piercing howl cut through the night. It came from the direction of the mill, and turned Ruby's shame into a chill of dread. "Is that…?"

"Hardulph," said Fillan, getting to his feet. "He's coming."

Ruby hauled herself upright. "We need to mask our scent. Quick, into the canal."

She made for the oily waters, but Fillan stopped her and pointed downstream. A small tugboat was labouring towards them, towing a long barge piled high with refuse. A cloud of flies hovered over it, as thick as smoke.

"A garbage scow?" she said.

"A free ride," he answered.

They retreated into the shadow of the nearby buildings until the barge had drawn near. It almost filled the canal from side to side, so they had no trouble breaking from cover and leaping the small gap into the steaming mounds of rotting food, broken furniture and unidentifiable sludge. Ruby sank in up to her knees and gagged with revulsion.

"Isn't it great?" said Fillan, beaming. "Not even Hardulph will be able to smell us in all this, *and* it's taking us out of the Narrows."

Ruby watched the canal banks creeping past. "It's taking us very *slowly*."

Another howl cut through the night, terrifyingly close, and she pulled him behind a mouldy old armchair as Hardulph's ghostly white form shot out onto the towpath. Holding her breath, Ruby risked a peek and saw Hardulph sniffing the air, turning this way and that as he scanned the shadows. She tried to duck back out of sight but was too slow – his eyes locked on hers.

"We're in trouble," she whispered.

At that instant, a dazzling beam of light lanced down from the sky. It swept from one side of the canal to the other, painting the water as bright as day, and settled on Hardulph. The great wolf threw up an arm to shield his eyes, but another searchlight snapped on, and then a third.

"You there!" boomed a voice from on high. "Stay where you are!"

"Breck?" said Fillan.

He and Ruby looked up as, with a roar of engines,

something like a huge silver torpedo slid into view over the nearest houses. It was a police airship, and the gondola on its underside bristled with lights, telescopes and rapid-fire crossbows, and it had Hardulph pinned in its searchlights.

"I never thought I'd be pleased to see the NCPD again," said Ruby.

"Paws where we can see them!" bellowed Breck through the airship's loudspeaker. "You're under arrest for associating with the Tooth and Claw killers. Officers are on their way to—"

Before he could finish, Hardulph took a loping step towards the barge. A hail of crossbow bolts shattered against the cobblestones at the wolf's feet.

"I said freeze!" roared Breck.

Hardulph shot Ruby a look of pure fury, before turning on the spot and racing away into the darkened streets. More crossbow bolts sparked and pinged off the road behind him.

"After him!" demanded Breck, and the airship hummed into motion again.

Ruby and Fillan watched it disappear over the Narrows, its lights tracing the winding streets.

"That was too close," said Ruby, slumping against the armchair.

"Agreed," said Fillan. "But hopefully Breck will keep Hardulph busy for a while."

"Which gives us time to track down Charlotte Grimm. She can tell us what we need to know. Come on."

Fillan shook his head. "Can we stay here for a bit? I'm exhausted."

Ruby stood, and tried to pull Fillan up with her, only to realize that her bones felt as heavy as cement. She flopped down beside him.

"You win," she said.

They huddled together and watched the city slide by.

An hour later, the scow had left the northern end of the canal and ventured onto the choppier waters of the Fenris River. It was quiet here, the noise of the city softened to a distant hum.

Ruby watched the rainbow swirls on the river's oily surface, and wondered about Marceline. Was she alive? If she was, how badly hurt? Her guilt continued to gnaw at her, but with it came other questions, and she finally put one of them to Fillan.

"If Marceline didn't kill Alarick, who did?"

"I don't know," he replied. "But the more I think about it, the more I wonder if his death is linked to the paper mill somehow. It was a big secret for him and Marceline to be keeping."

Ruby considered this. It certainly seemed logical. "She said Alarick gave it to her as an apology."

"That's right."

"But they can't have made up. I'd know about it. Heck, everyone in the city would know."

Fillan thought on this for a moment. "They didn't sound very friendly at the press conference this morning. I could hear them from the corridor."

A memory intruded on Ruby's thoughts – the momentary quiver of Marceline's lip when she had broken the news of Alarick's death in the locker room that morning. Ruby had written it off as her imagination. But what if it hadn't been? Could Marceline and Alarick really have rekindled their friendship without telling anyone? In short, had they lied to the world? To *her*?

The idea was unsettling, so she banished it. "What sort of an apology is a ruined old building anyway?" she asked. "It's more like an insult."

"It has something to do with the future of Tooth and Claw, so it must be important," said Fillan.

"Important enough for someone to try to steal the deeds," Ruby replied.

Fillan looked away quickly, and she knew he was

thinking about the bite he had inflicted on the intruder's hand. She hurried to change the subject.

"We should focus on finding Charlotte. Marceline said she knows what's going on."

"Who is she?"

"A sports reporter. She was outside Marceline's apartment this evening."

"Can we trust her?"

"Marceline thinks so." She watched the distant lights of the police airship, still roving over the Narrows. "What about that Hardulph? What's his deal?"

Fillan directed a dark look out across the water. "He said someone sent him. It obviously wasn't the NCPD, which means somebody else out there is after us."

"Somebody wants us dead, you mean," said Ruby. "Maybe it's Alarick's killer. They want Hardulph to stop us before we can uncover the truth."

They watched a seagull bob past with a limp hot dog in its beak. It eyed them jealously until it passed out of sight.

"All the more reason to find Charlotte," said Fillan. "Where does she work?"

"The *Netherburg Gazette*, but I don't know where their offices are. And even if I did, we can't just walk into a building full of journalists – we're trying to keep a low profile, remember?"

They pondered their predicament in silence, until the tone of the tug's engine shifted. The boat was slowing, and pulling towards the river's western bank. Peering over the mound of refuse, Ruby saw a couple of men wheeling an overflowing dumpster to the end of a jetty up ahead.

"Looks like we're taking on more garbage," she said.

As they approached the jetty, the tugboat captain opened the cabin door and set about readying the mooring line. As he did so, a tinny voice drifted out of the cabin from an old portable radio.

"…search for the Tooth and Claw killers continues following the vicious attack at the Peterson Paper Mill earlier this evening. Reports of a second wolf at the scene remain unconfirmed, but the victim, celebrated Tooth and Claw coach Marceline Plats, suffered severe injuries and has been rushed, unconscious and in critical condition, to Saint Gummarus's Hospital."

Ruby had to bite down a scream of excitement. "Marceline's alive!" she whispered. "We have to get there."

"To the hospital?" Fillan's eyebrows rose. "That's a terrible idea – the police are bound to be there too. And what about finding Charlotte?"

"She'll probably be there covering the story. And we can avoid the police. It's not like they'll be expecting us."

They grabbed the armchair for support as the barge bumped against the jetty, and they heard the captain exchange a few words with the men on shore as he made fast the mooring line.

With a lot of grunting and complaining, the team on the jetty began upending the dumpster onto the barge. An avalanche of tin cans, glass bottles and rotten cabbages rained down.

"I guess it's worth a shot," said Fillan. "And it'll smell better."

They waited until the captain had unmoored and the workmen had wheeled the dumpster back into the city. Then, as the boat pulled slowly away, they scrambled over the heap of rubbish and jumped off onto the jetty.

"But if there's any sign of trouble, we leave," said Fillan. "Agreed?"

Ruby steeled herself. The city still felt like a giant trap, poised to spring closed on them, but they had a new goal now – find Charlotte Grimm and convince her to tell them what she knew about the paper mill. It wasn't much, but it was a thread of hope, and Ruby was determined to follow it as far as she could.

"Agreed," she finally said. "And relax. I'm sure the worst is behind us."

Hardulph was angry. Twice he had let his prey slip between his paws. It was all the fault of that interfering woman, with her twisted leg and stinging cane. He rubbed his jaw where it had raised a nasty welt beneath the fur. She had fought surprisingly well, and it had taken all his strength to finally overcome her. Then the flying machines had arrived, with their lights and weapons. They hunted him like cowards, safe in the skies, until he had finally given them the slip.

Now he had his quarry's scent again – or rather, the stench of the foul river craft on which they had hidden – and he cut a neat wake through the waters of the Fenris, following them south. He was a strong swimmer, and their boat moved slowly. He would be with them again soon, and then they would pay for humiliating him.

But right now he was hungry. He spied a seagull floating on the scummy waters, a sausage in its beak.

Hardulph slipped beneath the surface and dived deep. Then he turned, and rocketed up from below. A snap of his jaws, a crunch of bones, and both seagull and wiener were gone.

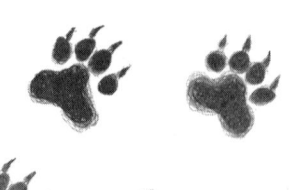

CHAPTER 17
Critical Care

Saint Gummarus's Hospital was an imposing complex of white stone buildings clustered around an art deco tower on the western banks of the Fenris. A police cordon was in place around the ambulance bay, and a scrum of reporters had gathered outside it by the time Ruby and Fillan stole into the darkened park across the street and peered out through the railings.

"There's no way we're getting in there," said Fillan.

Ruby scowled, unwilling to admit defeat so soon. "I told you Charlotte Grimm would be here though." She pointed to the telltale red trilby, visible at the heart of the crowd.

"How are we going to reach her?"

Ruby scanned the busy street, searching for inspiration.

The western half of the city was wealthier than the east, and it showed. The street was broad, tree-lined and busy with trams and motor cars. Even getting close to the hospital without being spotted was going to be a challenge, let alone getting through the crowd to Charlotte.

As she watched, one of the trams drew to a halt just outside the park and disgorged a horde of people who shouted and chattered and cajoled.

It was Akako's family, just as animated as they'd been outside the press room that morning. Akako was almost lost in their midst, walking silently with her hood up and head down.

It was all Ruby could do not to call to her. Instead, she melted into the shadows as the group approached, cupped her hands around her mouth and gave a hooting whistle. None of the adults seemed to notice, but Akako looked up sharply as she passed.

"What are you doing?" whispered Fillan, shrinking into the bushes.

"Trust me," Ruby replied.

She watched Akako take her mother's hand and whisper something in her ear. Then the group crossed the street towards the hospital, leaving Akako behind. Akako pursed her lips and returned the wood pigeon call.

Beaming from ear to ear, Ruby slapped Fillan on the

shoulder and emerged from the shadows. "Akako. Try not to react. Just play it cool."

"It *is* you!" Despite the excitement in her voice, Akako leaned casually against the railings, hands in pockets, a bored expression on her face. "Are you okay? What are you doing here? And what's that terrible smell?"

"Long story," Ruby replied. "Are you here for Marceline?"

"Yes, isn't it terrible? We got the news about half an hour ago. I told my mum I'd wait here for the others."

Ruby's pulse quickened. "Voss and Roselyn are coming?"

Akako nodded. "The police said Marceline was attacked by that wolf boy you escaped with."

"It wasn't me!"

Akako's composure faltered as Fillan stepped out of the shadows and, despite the heavy iron railings between them, she retreated a few steps.

"He's telling the truth," said Ruby. "We were with Marceline when it happened, but Fillan had nothing to do with it. There's another wolf after us."

Akako looked aghast. "Why is all this happening, Rubes?"

Ruby was prevented from answering when a sleek black automobile pulled up at the kerb nearby. She and Fillan ducked back out of sight as a man and woman emerged, dressed in expensive-looking evening wear – Roselyn's parents. Roselyn appeared next, wearing a floor-length blood-red dress, matching gloves and a clutch bag. At the same time, Voss – dressed in a faded denim midi-dress and jacket – appeared from the other direction, chattering nervously with her brothers.

"Give me a minute," said Akako. As the two groups converged, she hurried over and drew Roselyn and Voss into a huddle, away from their families.

"This is risky," whispered Fillan.

"I know," Ruby replied. "But we need all the friends we can get right now."

She watched Roselyn return to her parents while Voss slunk back to her brothers. After brief, murmured conversations, the families crossed the road to the hospital, leaving the girls behind.

"Why exactly do we need an emergency team meeting in the street?" said Roselyn.

Akako propped herself against the railings again. "Maybe I should let Ruby explain."

Taking her cue, Ruby emerged from the shadows with Fillan. "Hi," she said.

Voss recoiled. "Whoa!" She turned in a quick circle, checking nervously about. "I mean, it's good to see you, Rubes, but you two are Netherburg's most wanted."

Roselyn was more contained. "What's your strategy here, Ruby? There's an army of reporters across the street. Do you know what will happen if they see us together?"

"I'm sorry, but we need your help."

Voss continued to turn in anxious circles until Roselyn put a steadying hand on her shoulder.

"Let's hear it," said Roselyn.

"Thanks," said Ruby. "Nice dress, by the way."

"Oh, this?" Roselyn waved the compliment away. "My parents arranged a party to celebrate what was *supposed* to be our big win today."

Akako looked at her sideways. "You've been celebrating after everything that's happened?"

"Of course not, but Daddy had already paid for everything, so he insisted we go ahead. Then we got the call about Marceline." She looked pointedly at Ruby. "The police say you two were there."

"Yes, but it's not like that," said Ruby. "Someone hired a wild wolf to track us down. He attacked us. Marceline fought him off." To her own surprise, a tear spilled down her cheek, cutting a trail through the layer of grime. She wiped it away, embarrassed. "We wouldn't be here without her."

Roselyn's eyes narrowed. "It sounds like *she* wouldn't be in the hospital without *you*."

The words stung so sharply that Ruby gasped.

"Ros!" said Akako, shocked.

"I'm sorry, Ruby," said Roselyn. "I know you didn't kill Alarick, but this wouldn't have happened to Marceline if you hadn't gone on the run."

"If we hadn't, we'd both be in a jail cell right now, and nobody would be looking for the real killer," Ruby shot back.

"Do you think you're the only person in the whole city who can solve this?" said Roselyn. "Or that we'd all just abandon you?"

Ruby's face prickled with a mix of shame and anger. Ever since she'd escaped the police in the bowels of the stadium, she'd assumed she was on her own – responsible for keeping Fillan safe and clearing both their names. Perhaps Marceline had been right about her after all. "I can't solve this without your help, Ros. All of you. We need to speak to Charlotte Grimm. She's right across the street."

"Why?" asked Roselyn.

Fillan spoke up. "Because Marceline was hiding the truth about her and Alarick. They were working together on something big, and Charlotte has the details."

He lapsed into an awkward silence as Roselyn, Voss and Akako exchanged doubtful looks.

"Marceline would never work with Alarick," said Voss.

"But she did," said Ruby. "She told us herself."

Voss and Akako both looked to Roselyn, who stared down Fillan until his ears went flat.

"If that's true, then everything we've been working towards for the past year has been a lie," she said. "Do you really think Marceline would do that to us?"

It was a good question and, looking at the nervous expressions on her friends' faces, Ruby could tell that they were as unsettled by it as she was. "I hope not," she replied. "But Charlotte can tell us for sure."

All eyes swung back to Roselyn. She tapped her foot. She pursed her lips. "No," she replied finally. "I'm sorry, Ruby, but we can't help you."

"Why not?" said Ruby in disbelief.

"Because this situation is already out of control," said Roselyn. "You're filthy, you've got no plan, and people are getting hurt."

"I've told you the plan," said Ruby. "We're here to speak to Charlotte."

"And then what?" said Roselyn.

"How should I know?"

Roselyn arched a perfectly shaped eyebrow and, with a horrible sinking feeling, Ruby realized she had just lost the argument.

"You're dragging the team's reputation through the mud," said Roselyn. "There's already talk of them banning us from next year's tournament. The longer you run, the more trouble you cause."

"We're running *away* from trouble," said Ruby, without much conviction.

"What about the reports of an attack in Marceline's apartment building? Was that a wild wolf too?" Roselyn looked at Fillan, who shrank under her gaze.

"I didn't mean to," he said.

Roselyn turned back to Ruby. "Are you sure he's even safe to be around?"

Ruby grabbed the railings with both hands, as if she could bend them apart and thrust her face through the gap. "I thought you were on my side."

"I'm on the team's side," Roselyn replied. "That's why I'm telling you to hand yourself in before things get any worse."

Ruby set her jaw. "Not gonna happen."

"Then I'm sorry, but you leave me no choice," said Roselyn. "You're no longer a member of the Netherburg Reds."

CHAPTER 18
Friends and Enemies

Ruby staggered back from the park railings as if they had delivered an electric shock. Roselyn's words rang in her ears, and she saw her disbelief mirrored in the faces of Voss and Akako. "Only Marceline has the authority to kick me off the team," she said.

"She can't do anything, thanks to you," said Roselyn. "That leaves me in charge, and if you won't listen to your captain, you're not a true Red."

Ruby was gathering a particularly choice insult to hurl back at her when Akako intervened.

"Let's all calm down for a second," she said. "Ros, if Grimm knows something that could clear Ruby's name, don't you think we should hear it?"

Roselyn's cheeks flushed. "I've already made my decision."

"The *wrong* decision," said Fillan.

"You don't get a say in this," snapped Roselyn.

"Do I?" asked Ruby. Angry tears welled in her eyes.

"Come with us and hand yourself in," said Roselyn. "You'll be safe from that wild wolf, and we'll back you up all the way. Daddy knows some very good lawyers."

"We don't need lawyers," said Ruby. "We need to know who killed Alarick."

Roselyn sighed. "You're just making this harder for everyone." She drew a perfume bottle from her clutch bag and spritzed herself with it. "Remember what Marceline always taught us – play to win, but know when you've lost."

"I am *not* going to lose this!" Ruby balled her fists, ready to reach through the railings and shake Roselyn by the throat until her earrings rattled. The only thing that stopped her was the tickle of Fillan's nose against her ear as he leaned in close.

"Rose water," he whispered.

"What?"

He sniffed, catching the last droplets of Roselyn's perfume as they dispersed on the breeze. "I was wrong. It wasn't Wild Wood Roses I smelled in Marceline's apartment. It was rose water."

He nodded towards Roselyn, and Ruby's eyes widened in sudden understanding.

"Ros," she said, rubbing her tears away with her palms. "You're right-handed, aren't you?"

"What's that got to do with anything?"

"It's just that you're holding your bag in your left hand."

Roselyn stiffened. "I can use any hand I like."

"Of course." Ruby nodded. "But why not your right?"

Roselyn said nothing, but was unable to hide the flicker in her eyes. Akako and Voss, meanwhile, watched on in confusion.

"Is your hand okay?" asked Ruby.

"It's fine," said Roselyn. Slowly and deliberately, she transferred the bag from her left hand to her right. The twinge of discomfort at the corner of her lips was very slight, but it was all Ruby needed.

"Take the glove off," she said.

"Marceline needs us," Roselyn replied. "Come on, team."

She turned to leave, but Ruby threw herself at the railings and caught Roselyn's bag.

"It was you in Marceline's apartment!" she said.

Roselyn yanked the bag free, scattering a handkerchief and a tube of lipstick across the pavement, and sending Ruby sprawling onto her back. "You're delusional."

Fillan helped Ruby back to her feet. "You stole the deeds to the paper mill," he said. "How did you know about it? What were Marceline and Alarick planning?"

Shock and fear vied for supremacy in Roselyn's expression, until she locked them away behind a mask of cold indifference. "I have no idea what you're talking about. Voss? Akako? With me."

"Wait." Akako caught her arm. "Is any of this true?"

Roselyn looked at her sharply. "Don't make me kick you off the team as well."

She stalked away across the street, weaving through the traffic with barely a glance. Voss scrambled to pick up Roselyn's scattered items, dropped them in a fluster, and hurried after her, shamefaced.

Akako picked up the mess and stuffed it into her hoodie pockets. "Are you sure it was her?"

"Yes," said Ruby. "I don't know why, but she's mixed up in this somehow. *Please* believe us."

Akako shuffled from foot to foot, deep in thought. "Let me talk to her again," she said. "Maybe I can bring her around." With that, she crossed the road towards the hospital.

Ruby slumped onto the grass. She felt hollow and utterly defeated. "I can't believe it," she said. "My own teammates."

Fillan put an arm around her shoulders. "I'm sorry."

There was a sudden commotion across the street. Cars braked and horns blared as the crowd of reporters moved as one, rushing towards the park. On the hospital steps beyond them, Ruby could just make out Roselyn, pointing in their direction.

"I don't believe it!" Ruby cried. "She's ratted us out!"

CHAPTER 19
Meet the Press

Ruby and Fillan retreated into the cover of the bushes as the crowd of reporters reached the park railings.

"Ruby Calvino, are you in there?"

"Did you really attack your own coach?"

Flashbulbs went off like a lightning storm, illuminating the patch of earth where Ruby and Fillan had been standing. When they saw that it was empty, the reporters stampeded along the pavement, hunting for a way in.

"We need to go," said Fillan.

Ruby stumbled after him, numb with shock. "My own team," she said. "How could they do this to me?"

"To us, you mean."

They headed deeper into the park, but the darkened lawns and pathways were already filling with running figures as the press streamed in through the gates. The mob were loud and uncoordinated, but they were enough to jog Ruby out of her own head.

"Keep low," she whispered. "We can sneak past them as long as we don't draw attention to ourselves."

The moment she said it, a dazzling flash froze them both to the spot. "They're here!" The photographer had crept up behind them, and was now waving frantically. He raised his camera, ready for another shot, but Ruby lunged at him. He panicked and fell backwards, discharging the flash into the sky.

"So much for not drawing attention," said Fillan as he and Ruby raced past the man and into a tunnel of climbing roses.

"Stop complaining and keep running," Ruby shot back. There were shouts and running footsteps converging from all angles now, as the press pack closed in.

A figure appeared at the end of the rose tunnel, blocking their path. Ruby prepared to barge them out of the way until she recognized them. "Akako?"

"This way," said Akako, and pulled them both into a stand of rhododendrons. They crouched together in the dirt as several people rushed past. "Sorry," Akako whispered. "Ros put the press onto your scent before I could even try to talk her around."

Ruby hissed. "I knew it!"

"So I quit the Reds," said Akako. "Sign me up for Team Ruby."

Ruby blinked back unexpected tears as she took both Akako's hands in hers. "Thank you."

"What do you need?" asked Akako.

"A distraction, so we can get away."

Akako thought for a moment. "If they think I'm you, I can lead them away from the gates so you can slip out."

"Good idea. We're almost the same size – let's swap clothes."

Fillan peered out through the foliage as Ruby squirmed out of the flannel shirt and flat cap that the old man in Marceline's apartment building had given them. "What about Charlotte Grimm?" he asked. "We still need to speak with her."

"We can't speak with anyone if we're caught," said Ruby. "We'll figure something out later."

"But we might not get another chance."

Ruby pulled Akako's hoodie on. For an instant it felt good to be back in red, until she remembered that Roselyn had kicked her off the team. She burned with bitter resentment. "Are you ready?"

Akako finished buttoning the old man's shirt and

nodded. "It won't take them long to figure out I'm not you though."

"We'll be quick," said Ruby. "Good luck."

"You too," said Akako. "And just so you know, I don't blame you for what happened to Marceline. So go and find who *is* responsible."

She pulled the cap down over her hair, shot out of the bush, and disappeared into the night.

"There she is!" someone shouted. "After her!"

The cry was taken up across the park, and several reporters pounded past the rhododendrons in pursuit.

"Ready?" Ruby steeled herself for a sprint, only for Fillan to put a restraining hand on her arm.

"We can't leave without speaking to Charlotte."

She shook herself free. "We don't have time for this. If we don't leave now, we'll never get away."

She didn't wait for him, but burrowed out of the bush and took off in a low, loping run across the nearest lawn. Ten metres to her left, the reporters were trampling a bed of irises as they encircled a beech tree, shouting and elbowing each other aside to get close to it. She soon saw why – Akako had climbed into the branches.

Ruby signalled Fillan to follow her, and was about to move on when she spotted the bright red of Charlotte Grimm's coat. Charlotte hadn't joined the fray at the base of the tree, but was hanging back at the rear of the group, pacing slowly back and forth, notebook at the ready.

Giving herself more time and room to react if Akako makes it past the others, Ruby thought. *Smart move.*

Fillan joined her. "Aren't we going?" he whispered. "If any of them turn around…"

Ruby pointed to Charlotte. "You were right, we need to find out what she knows. You take cover, I'm going to go over there and speak to her."

"Someone's bound to see you if you try it here," he said. "We need somewhere more private."

"Like where?" she said. "Should we invite her back to the bush?"

He gave her a deadpan look. "Akako put Roselyn's handkerchief in her pocket. Is it still there?"

Ruby gave an exasperated sigh but turned out the pockets of Akako's hoodie. "Yes," she said, holding it up. "And her lipstick. Why?"

He took them from her, spread the handkerchief out on the grass and scribbled a note on it with the lipstick:

The Hungry Pup. One hour. Come alone.

"Can you get that into her pocket?" he asked, handing her the note.

"What's the Hungry Pup?"

"I'll explain later. Just hurry before someone sees us."

Ruby locked her eyes on Charlotte. The park was suddenly an arena. There were hunters on the loose; she had her flag and had to reach her target. A *live* target.

She streaked across the lawn without a sound, coming up directly behind Charlotte and falling into step with her. They paced left and right in perfect unison for a few seconds before Ruby leaned in, close as a shadow, and slipped the handkerchief into the woman's coat pocket.

Her mission accomplished, she backed away to Fillan's side before Charlotte could turn and see her. "Now what?" she asked.

"Leave that to me," he replied.

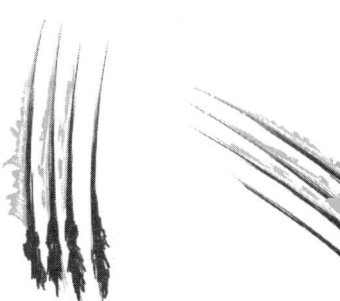

CHAPTER 20
The Hungry Pup

The park was forty minutes behind them when Fillan led Ruby onto a side street deep in the west of the city. It was very late now, and the pavements had emptied. Nevertheless, the drone of a police airship echoed off the buildings, and searchlights flashed through the night from the direction of the river.

Fillan drew to a halt in front of a darkened diner, fashioned from an old railway carriage parked between two office buildings. Red-and-white chequered curtains hung in the windows, and the neon sign on its roof, though not illuminated, was easy to make out – THE HUNGRY PUP.

"We'll use the kitchen door," he said, leading her around the back of the structure. They squeezed past the trash cans into a small yard, where he fished under some upturned potted plants until he produced a key.

"Dad leaves this here because he's always locking himself out," he explained, unlocking the back door. "He thinks my mum and I don't know."

"Your parents work here?" said Ruby, surprised.

"It's the family business," he said, and ushered her inside.

The kitchen was narrow and dark, with a small hatch opening onto the dining area at the front of the carriage. Fillan led her through and they slid into a booth overlooking the street. Just enough light spilled in from outside for Ruby to look around and take in the interior.

It was cosy and clean, decorated in black, white and red, with flowers in small glass vases on each table to add some scent. Framed photos above the lunch counter depicted a male and female wolf, both wearing aprons, posing proudly with Fillan in front of the diner, working in the kitchen, and seated at the counter, drinking milkshakes.

"You really do want to be a chef," she said.

"Of course," he replied. "I've been helping Mum and Dad out for years, but I really want to open my own place. Five stars. The best in the whole city."

She smiled. "Do it, and I'll be your first customer."

"Roast beef sandwich with all the trimmings?"

"You remembered." Then a sudden realization hit her. "But you're vegetarian! And I bought you a raw lamb chop at Fangbrook. I'm so sorry. No wonder you didn't eat it."

He shrugged. "You were only trying to help, and it smelled fresh. Maybe I should find out who their supplier is."

"From what I overheard, it's probably the Oma Gang."

Fillan's mouth dropped open. "The crime ring? I told you that place was bad news."

"At least that's one problem we don't have to deal with." Ruby drummed her fingers on the laminated tabletop. "Do you think Charlotte will come?"

"She's already here."

The voice from the kitchen made them both start. Framed by the serving hatch, her elbows on the counter, was Charlotte Grimm. She held up Roselyn's handkerchief with the lipstick note on it, now rather smeared.

"Sorry to startle you, but when I get a cryptic invitation to a secret meeting in the middle of the night, I figure I'm expected to sneak in through the back." She stuffed the handkerchief into her pocket. "This had better be good."

Fillan arrived at the table carrying a tray loaded with food. "Veggie hot dogs, fries, onion rings and three ice cream sundaes," he announced.

Ruby's eyes lit up at the sight. "Amazing." She had taken the time to wash up in the diner's small restroom, and even patched her wound with a bandage from a first-aid kit in the kitchen.

Charlotte, meanwhile, sat on the bench opposite Ruby, peering out at the street from between the curtains, which were now closed. "I hope you realize the risk I'm taking here," she said. "You two are a hot ticket right now. Breck would slap me in handcuffs and throw away the key just for talking to you."

"We know the feeling," Ruby replied. "But there are some questions we really need to ask you."

"Me first," said Charlotte. "Did you murder Alarick?"

"No," Ruby replied. "And we didn't attack Marceline."

"In fact, she sent us to you," added Fillan, sliding onto the bench beside Ruby.

Charlotte's eyebrows rose. "Interesting." She pulled a notebook and pen from inside her coat and flipped the notebook open. "Start at the beginning, and don't skip a thing."

It took half an hour for them to recount everything that had happened since their first meeting in the Hunter's

Den. By the time they had finished, both their stomachs and Charlotte's notebook were a lot fuller. She flipped the book shut, sat back, and stared hard at them both.

"I knew something smelled fishy," she said.

"That's probably us," said Fillan. "We're also cabbagey, but I promise I washed my hands before handling the food."

"No, I mean this whole situation stinks of a set-up," Charlotte replied. "I just couldn't be certain until I'd heard your side of the story."

Ruby leaned forward, planting her elbows on the table. "Now that we've shared everything *we* know, what can you tell us about the paper mill? Marceline said there's a plan, and whatever it is, we're certain it has something to do with Alarick's murder."

Charlotte picked the last remaining onion ring from her plate and took a bite. "The plan was supposed to be a secret. Until tomorrow."

"Why, what happens tomorrow?" asked Fillan.

"That's when Marceline and Alarick were going to take the whole thing public. Their secret friendship, the paper mill, everything. I've had the press release typed and ready for weeks. It was going to be the biggest story of the year."

Ruby squirmed impatiently. "Tell us!"

Charlotte finished the onion ring with a decisive crunch. "They planned to convert the mill into the best Tooth and Claw training centre in the country. All the latest equipment. Artificial turf. A new, retractable roof. Flood lighting. Fully climate controlled. A place to nurture the raw talent from the Narrows and give it a real home."

Ruby sat back in disbelief. She'd never dreamed of anything so wonderful before, but now that Charlotte had painted the picture, she wanted it more than anything.

"Is that why Alarick bought the mill?" asked Fillan.

Charlotte nodded. "It was a childhood dream that he and Marceline cooked up when they were still playing in the streets, but it died when they had their falling-out."

"Alarick's apology," said Ruby. "So that's what Marceline meant – he bought the building for her to prove that he was really sorry."

Charlotte cinched her mouth into a half smile. "I don't know if it makes up for everything he did to her, but it sure beats flowers and a box of chocolates."

Fillan paused, a scoop of ice cream halfway to his mouth, dripping chocolate sauce onto the table. "So the plan wasn't anything sinister at all. Alarick was doing something nice."

"It would have transformed the Narrows," said Charlotte. "New jobs, new investment. Teams would have come from all over the country to train there. I'd have loved to have something like that when I was a kid."

"You played Tooth and Claw?" asked Ruby.

"Five years for the Riverside Runners," said Charlotte, with the ghost of a smile. "We never got to the finals, but it was fun while it lasted."

"Why did you stop?" asked Fillan.

The smile faded. "There was no real future in it for me. The *Gazette*'s sports desk was hiring. The rest is history."

Doubt began to gnaw at Ruby's excitement. "If Alarick was building a new training centre, then it can't have been the reason for his murder," she said. "The whole city would benefit, so why kill him for it?"

"That's the question," said Charlotte. "Maybe your friend Roselyn has some answers."

The thought of Roselyn twisted in Ruby's chest like a knife, and she had to gather her courage before she could speak again. "I don't know what to think about Ros right now."

"*I* think she's mixed up in something very bad," said Charlotte. "The only people in Netherburg who were supposed to know about the training centre were Marceline, Alarick and me. So why was Roselyn after those plans?"

"Someone must have told her about them," said Fillan.

"Not me," said Charlotte. "I'd never risk blowing my big story."

"And she never spoke to Alarick," said Ruby. "So it must have been Marceline."

Charlotte sucked in her cheeks. "She didn't tell any of the rest of you. And even if she did tell Roselyn, why steal the plans?"

Ruby examined the question from every direction she could think of, but couldn't arrive at an answer. Then Fillan spoke up.

"Maybe she was stealing them for someone else."

They all looked at each other.

"It could be another journalist, trying to undermine my scoop," said Charlotte. "They might have offered her plenty of cash."

Ruby shook her head. "Ros doesn't need money – her parents are loaded. She must have another reason."

Silence settled over them, broken only by the clink of Fillan's spoon in the depths of his sundae glass. Then he sat up, suddenly alert.

"There's something we haven't thought of," he said. "The money to buy the paper mill and convert it into the training centre. A project that big isn't cheap, and Marceline isn't exactly rich. So where were the funds coming from?"

"From Alarick," said Charlotte. "He borrowed a fortune to finance the whole thing."

Ruby cocked an eyebrow. "Why did he need to borrow it? Hadn't he already made a fortune from Tooth and Claw?"

Charlotte chuckled. "Sure, and he'd spent it all, several times over. He was constantly in debt."

Ruby reflected on the imported scent sticks and the hand-reared pork chops in the Hunter's Den. Everyone in Netherburg knew that Alarick lived in the largest mansion in the exclusive Hillsborough District – a far cry from the life of a Narrows street urchin. "Who did he borrow the money from?" she asked.

"A good question," Charlotte replied. "Most of the banks had cut him off because he owed them so much."

Ruby sifted through the fragments of knowledge they'd gathered, and one stood out clearly. "'Pay your dues'," she said. "What if the poisoned roses weren't sent by a rival at all? What if they were from whoever lent him the money?"

Fillan's tail wagged, slapping against the inside of the booth. "If he hadn't repaid his debt, they might have decided to kill him."

"It's something to go on, at least," said Charlotte. "Was the note signed?"

"No," said Ruby. "There was just a logo. A rose inside a house. And it was all gold."

Charlotte grinned, triumphant. "In that case, I know exactly where we need to go."

CHAPTER 21
Say It with Flowers

The Hillsborough District was built, as the name implied, on the slopes of Netherburg's only hill. It was as much a park as a neighbourhood, with lawns and gardens spilling down the hillside from the grand houses at the summit. At the foot of the hill was a cobbled plaza of small, exclusive shops, overhung with wisteria and ivy. They were dark and shuttered now, except for one.

"The Flower Haus," said Charlotte, drawing her car up to the plaza's entrance. "They did the flowers for my cousin's wedding last year. Cost her a fortune. Very exclusive."

Ruby and Fillan peered out from the car's back seat. The shopfront was painted white and gold, and the windows were filled with a rainbow of bouquets. A single light burned inside, illuminating the sign above the door: a golden rose within the outline of a house.

"This is definitely where the roses that killed Alarick came from," said Fillan. "If we can get inside, we might find a record of who ordered them."

Hope stirred in Ruby, but she couldn't ignore a nagging doubt. "Why do they have a light on in the middle of the night?"

"Maybe someone forgot to switch it off," said Charlotte.

Ruby and Fillan climbed out of the car, nervous to be in the open again.

"Sorry I can't stay," said Charlotte, leaning out of the window. "My editor's waiting for my story on the paper mill attack, and my neck's on the line if I don't turn something in. But here." She produced a business card from the glove compartment and handed it over. "That's my office number. If you get stuck, call me."

Ruby slipped the card into her pocket. "Thanks," she said. "We need all the friends we can get right now."

"You're going to have more friends than you can count once we break this story wide open," Charlotte replied. "The whole of Netherburg's going to see the truth." With a final wave, she pulled away into the night.

As her car's engine faded into the distance, Ruby and

Fillan dashed across the plaza to the shop and peered in through the windows.

"It looks deserted," said Ruby. "We just need to find a way in."

They started examining the door but were interrupted by the roar of an approaching car. Ruby knew instantly that it wasn't Charlotte's – the sound was deeper, like a throaty growl.

"Quick!"

A row of large privet bushes stood in pots along the pavement, and she and Fillan ducked behind one as the car swept into the plaza, its headlights painting the sleeping buildings. It was a big, expensive machine with long art deco fins, and it pulled to a stop outside the Flower Haus. Two people alighted from the rear seats and exchanged a word with the driver – a chauffeur, Ruby guessed – before the car pulled away again.

The light from the shop lit them clearly, and Ruby had to clamp a hand over her mouth to suppress her gasp of shock. Roselyn's parents!

They walked without hesitation to the door, pushed it open, and stepped inside.

"It was unlocked all along," said Fillan. He and Ruby scurried back to the shop, keeping low, and peeked in through the windows. "Do we follow them?"

"Of course," she said.

As slowly and quietly as they could, they eased the door open and slipped inside.

The shop's interior was decorated in white and gold, and dotted with huge vases that overflowed with tropical flowers. In the half-light, they provided ideal cover, and the sharp clacking of Roselyn's mother's stilettos against the tiled floor masked the sound of their footsteps.

From their hiding places, Ruby and Fillan watched the pair walk to the back of the shop. As if out of thin air, a sleek grey wolf appeared from behind a large cactus and intercepted them. She wore a Flower Haus apron and carried a clipboard.

"Names?" she said.

Roselyn's father took a small step back, and his wife clutched his hand in both of hers. "You know perfectly well who we are," he said. "Let us in."

"Names," the wolf replied.

"Mr and Mrs Brandt. Now hurry up, we don't have much time."

The wolf, however, seemed to have all the time in the world. "And the purpose of your visit?"

Ruby watched an angry red blotch creep up Mr Brandt's neck from inside his shirt. "Must we do this every time?"

"The shop's closed to customers," said the wolf. "Unless you're here for something...specific."

Mrs Brandt silenced her husband with a look before he could vent his frustration any further. "We're here for the flower-arranging class," she said.

The wolf consulted her clipboard. "We've been waiting for you. Follow me." She led them out of sight behind a rack of terracotta pots. There was a whisper, a click and the room fell silent.

Ruby waited a few seconds before breaking cover. The shop looked deserted. "Where did they go?"

"I don't know," Fillan replied. "But something tells me they're not really here for a flower-arranging class." He hurried to the shop counter and lifted a leather-bound ledger from underneath it. "This looks like a register of sales."

"Anything about Alarick in there?"

Fillan scoured the last few pages and shook his head. "Nothing. Perhaps whoever sent the bouquet didn't want a paper trail."

"All the more reason to find out what Ros's parents are up to."

At that instant, light blazed in through the windows as another car swung into the plaza. It roared to a stop outside, and the two of them only just had time to duck behind the counter before the shop door burst open.

"Kelina!"

It was a man's voice, and it tugged at Ruby's memory. Where had she heard it before? Crawling on her hands and knees, she poked her head out around the side of the counter.

Jarvin, the man she had seen confronting Breck in Fangbrook Market, stood in the middle of the room, surrounded by a halo of smoke from his cigar. With a cold shock, Ruby got a proper look at the yellow flower in his lapel – a Wild Wood Rose.

Jarvin tapped his foot impatiently until the female wolf reappeared. "Is everything ready?" he asked.

"The Brandts just arrived," she replied. "Everyone's waiting for you."

Jarvin pulled a face, as if he had just tasted something that disagreed with him. "The Brandts too? What's the mood like down there?"

"Hostile," Kelina replied. "You'd better not keep them waiting."

He stubbed the cigar out in the nearest vase and followed her to the rear of the shop. "This Alarick thing keeps getting worse for us," he said. Then there was the same whisper and click that Ruby had heard before, and silence returned.

"That cigar stinks," said Fillan, waving his hand in front of his nose. "And that's coming from someone who just spent half an evening on a garbage scow."

Ruby barely noticed the cloud of smoke as she ploughed through it towards the back of the shop. "I saw that man at the market, which means the Oma Gang are here." Her body trembled with excitement. "We're close to the answers we need, I know it."

Fillan's fur bristled. "Are we sure we want to find them? The Oma Gang are bad news, Ruby. Maybe we should just call Charlotte."

She ignored him, and started exploring the rear of the shop. There were no doors or windows, just rows of shelves, stacked with potted plants of varying sizes. "It's like they vanished," she said.

Fillan sighed, shut his eyes and sniffed tentatively. "Smells don't vanish." He approached the wall, letting his nose guide him. "They passed through here."

"How?"

"There must be a hidden door. Look for a switch."

He started lifting pots from the shelves. Ruby followed suit, until she found one that refused to budge.

"This one's fixed to the shelf," she said.

Fillan examined it, then gave it a twist. With a soft, familiar click, a section of the wall whispered open. A narrow corridor, richly decorated and carpeted, lay beyond.

"Amazing!" Ruby slipped through, impatient to get moving. "Where do you think it leads?"

"Somewhere dangerous, probably."

She reached out a hand and he took it. "Marceline wasn't scared of danger," she said, leading him. "Let's make her proud."

The park opposite Saint Gummarus's Hospital lay in darkness and silence. The reporters had long since left in pursuit of Akako, who had vaulted from the tree, over their heads, and hit the lawn running. They left only trampled flowers and muddy footprints behind, while Akako had left the old man's flat cap that Ruby had swapped with her. It had fallen from her head during her escape, and the reporters had trampled it underfoot without even noticing. It was barely recognizable now, flattened and shabby.

But it called to Hardulph.

He picked it up and turned it over, slowly inhaling its scent. He had been forced to move slowly and carefully since emerging from the river – this part of the city was busy and bright, and the police were everywhere. And his prey were cunning. The garbage stink of the boat still clung to them, but it smelled like every trash can and dumpster in the city, and he had almost lost their trail twice. But this? This was proof that he was on the right path.

He buried his snout in the hat's fabric and took a deeper sniff. There were three scents on this! An old man smell, clean and dry and faded. One of his targets, the girl Ruby – the fabric was soaked with her sweat and panic. And the scent of another girl. A new, more recent smell.

So, they were swapping clothes now, were they? Very clever. He smiled to himself in the darkness. This was turning into a true challenge. He would have to work hard to find his prey's scent again. But he knew that he was close.

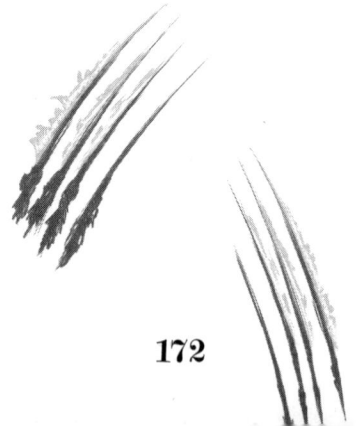

CHAPTER 22
The House Always Wins

Ruby and Fillan followed the secret hallway to a spiral staircase, which wound down into the Flower Haus's basement level. Music, laughter and raucous conversation drifted up from below.

"Sounds like someone's having a party," said Ruby.

"Under a flower shop?" said Fillan.

Treading softly, they descended the stairs and found themselves in a small cloakroom. Three walls were taken up with hats and coats, while the fourth was covered by a heavy red velvet curtain. The two friends eased it aside and peeped through.

A lavish hall lay before them, dripping with gold fittings and more red velvet. A jazz band played an up-tempo number from a stage at the far end, while the main floor was filled with men and women in evening wear. Pearls and sequins glittered. Silk shirts and cravats gleamed.

It certainly looked like a party, but the guests weren't paying any attention to the music. Instead, they crowded around a series of tables. Some played cards, others tossed dice, and, at a long table in the centre of the room, a group shouted and cheered as a man in a white uniform spun a horizontal wheel divided into red and black numbered slots.

"It's a casino!" Ruby whispered.

"But gambling's illegal in Netherburg," said Fillan.

"That's why it's run by the Oma Gang."

A waiter sailed past bearing a tray of cocktails, and they retreated behind the curtain.

"We can't go in there," said Fillan.

"We have to," Ruby replied. "That man, Jarvin, knows something about Alarick, and so do Ros's parents. If the Flower Haus is just a front for the Oma Gang, they must have had a hand in his murder."

"I'm more worried about them having a hand in *our* murders," said Fillan. "We can't just walk in and start asking questions."

"True." She looked around the room. Her training had taught her that, when your back was against the wall and you were sure there was no escape, you had to make use of whatever resources came to hand. Sometimes you could surprise even yourself. "I think I've got an idea," she said, a smile creeping across her face.

Fillan followed her gaze to the rows of coats. "Oh no," he said. "Not this again."

Few people paid attention to the gangling figure that lurched onto the casino floor from behind the curtain. He was a wolf in a trench coat and fedora, despite the heat. He was also unusually angular, as if the top half of his body was at odds with the lower half.

Ruby, who was the lower half in question, certainly felt at odds with Fillan, who was once again sitting on her shoulders. Trapped inside the coat, there was no escaping the rancid garbage smell that still clung to them both, or the sharp pain of her wound as Fillan's weight pushed down on it. She hoped they could get through all this quickly.

"A little to the left," Fillan whispered. "You're going to crash into the blackjack table."

"I'm trying my best," she hissed back.

She'd opened a slight gap between two of the coat's buttons, giving her a sliver of visibility. She negotiated her way around the table towards the centre of the room.

"Any sign of Jarvin?" she asked.

"Not yet," Fillan replied.

A figure stepped into their path, forcing Ruby to stop so suddenly that she almost pitched Fillan off her shoulders. It was Kelina the wolf.

"You're not one of our regulars," Kelina said. "Who are you?"

"Um…" said Fillan in a nervous squeak. "We're here… I mean, *I'm* here to see, um…"

Kelina looked them up and down with obvious suspicion. "Everyone on tonight's guest list has already signed in," she said. "And you're not on it."

Fillan tensed, digging his heels into Ruby's sides so sharply that she almost cried out. She began to panic. How had she ever imagined they would get away with this?

"Jarvin said I didn't need to sign in," said Fillan.

Ruby held her breath. Dropping Jarvin's name felt like a big risk, but it was enough to make Kelina pause.

"How do you know Jarvin?"

"From Fangbrook Market," said Fillan.

Kelina snorted. "That explains the smell, at least." She looked them over again, and wrinkled her nose. "Follow me. They've only just started."

Ruby was amazed. "Quick thinking," she whispered as she trotted in Kelina's wake.

"You must be rubbing off on me," Fillan replied.

Kelina led them to an offshoot of the hall, set apart from the casino floor by another red curtain. Stepping through it, they entered a dining room filled with circular wooden tables set for dinner. The occupants weren't eating though – they were on their feet, bellowing at Jarvin, who stood on one of the tables, shouting back.

"You people don't scare me," he said. "Remember who's in charge here!"

With a nod, Kelina withdrew, leaving Fillan and Ruby at the back of the throng.

"What's happening?" whispered Fillan.

"No idea," Ruby replied.

A woman in a purple sequined dress waved her handbag at Jarvin. "Who do you think you're kidding?" she yelled. "We're all here for the same thing. We want our money back! *All* of it!"

The group roared with approval.

"And I'm here to tell you, tough luck," Jarvin replied. "You all agreed to our terms when you placed your bets. If you win, we pay out. If you lose, we don't."

Roselyn's father climbed up on his chair. "But we didn't win *or* lose! Alarick died before the game finished, so the judges ruled the whole thing void."

"That's why you're only getting half your money back,"

said Jarvin. "Count yourselves lucky. If it were up to me, you'd get nothing at all."

Ruby momentarily forgot the weight of Fillan on her shoulders, and the terrible smell inside the coat. Roselyn's parents had placed an illegal bet on the Tooth & Claw final! Had Roselyn known? And had they betted for or against her?

"You've stolen six hundred of the florins I put on that game," said the woman in purple.

"And a thousand from me," shouted someone else.

"And *five* thousand from me!" cried Mr Brandt.

As the room descended into jeers and heckling, Ruby tapped Fillan on the shin. "This might be what we've been looking for."

"You think the Oma Gang killed Alarick so they could keep the betting money when the game was cancelled?"

"It would be a good motive, don't you think?"

Before he could answer, Jarvin silenced the crowd by drawing a compact crossbow from his jacket and firing three bolts into the ceiling in quick succession. People retook their seats as plaster rained down.

"Now you're getting it," said Jarvin. "If you don't like our rules, you can shut up and get out. Or if you're smart, you can stay and maybe win some of your money back at the tables. We're open all night. So, what'll it be?"

With a lot of grumbling and bitter looks, the people turned and shuffled towards the casino. All except the Brandts, who made a beeline for Jarvin. Ruby followed them, until she was close enough to eavesdrop.

"Please," Mr Brandt said. "You *have* to return my full bet. You don't know how much depends on it."

"And I don't care," said Jarvin, holstering his crossbow.

"It's our daughter's future," said Mrs Brandt. "We haven't told her, but the family business is failing. The ten thousand I wagered was the last of our savings."

Ruby's skin prickled. Roselyn had always been the rich kid, with the best of everything. Ruby had had no idea that the family was in so much trouble.

"We can loan you some cash if it means that much to you," said Jarvin. "But you'd better be able to pay it back, or there'll be consequences."

Mr Brandt stiffened. "I will not stoop to being bullied by a loan shark."

"Then this conversation is over," said Jarvin. "Enjoy being broke."

He left them standing pale and shaken, and shouldered past Ruby and Fillan on his way back to the casino floor. He had only taken a few steps past them when Kelina reappeared.

"Hey, Jarvin," she said. "You're supposed to tell me

when you invite your friends in."

Jarvin frowned. "What friends?"

Oh no, thought Ruby. With a sickening twist in her guts, she started looking for an escape route.

"This guy," said Kelina. "Your buddy from the market who smells like a dumpster."

Jarvin turned and narrowed his eyes at Fillan, who laughed nervously.

"I'm more of an acquaintance, really."

Slowly and calmly, Jarvin reached into his jacket and produced the crossbow again. "Here's what's gonna happen," he said, pressing the muzzle into what he assumed was Fillan's chest, but was actually Ruby's forehead. "You're gonna tell me who you are, and what you're doin' here, or I'm gonna turn your lungs into pincushions."

Ruby backed away, blinking nervous sweat from her eyes, but Kelina circled around to block them.

"P-please don't do anything you'll regret," stammered Fillan.

"Oh, *I'm* not gonna regret this," said Jarvin. He grabbed Fillan by the front of his coat, and Ruby made her move.

"Go!" She dropped out from beneath Fillan and rolled straight between Jarvin's legs. Without her to support him, Fillan dropped down through the coat, hit the ground and scampered away, leaving Jarvin holding the empty garment.

"What the…?" Jarvin looked between the two retreating figures. "Grab 'em!"

Ruby raced into the casino, weaving through the startled crowd. Kelina was close behind her, barging people aside until she was close enough to throw herself at Ruby in a clumsy tackle.

"Alarick would be embarrassed for you," said Ruby, springing onto the long table with the spinning wheel. Patrons screamed and grabbed for their winnings as she dashed across it, sending betting chips flying. She vaulted over the wheel and off the other side. Kelina leaped after her, only to plant her foot on the wheel and pitch head first into the man running the game. Players fell on the scattered chips, fighting to stuff their pockets.

Fillan, meanwhile, dived under one of the card tables as Jarvin rushed after him.

"Outta my way!" Jarvin roared, shoving people aside. Drinks spilled, glasses smashed and one man shoved back at him, hard. Jarvin felled him with a blow from the butt of his crossbow, only to have a champagne bottle smashed over his head by the man's girlfriend. Within seconds, the crowd at the table had turned into a brawling mob, and Fillan crawled between their legs on his stomach.

By the time he reached Ruby at the exit, the whole casino had descended into a riot. An elderly lady in pearls swung her handbag like a mace, walloping several young men across the face. Two men in tuxedos tried to throttle each other with their bow ties. The waiters had taken shelter behind a bar at one end of the room, and were lobbing bottles of seltzer at anyone who got too close. Even the jazz band had started battering each other with their instruments.

And ploughing through it all towards them, like a shark towards its prey, came Jarvin. His face was puce with rage, and his hair was dripping with champagne.

"Time to go," said Fillan.

They pulled aside the curtain to the cloakroom, only to find themselves face to face with Detective Breck.

"Finally," he said, levelling his crossbow at them. "You're under arrest."

CHAPTER 23
The Wrong Arm of the Law

Police officers piled out of the cloakroom from behind Breck, quickly surrounding Ruby and Fillan. Dozens more spread out across the casino, throwing themselves into the brawl and pulling the combatants apart. Ruby caught a glimpse of Jarvin turning on his heel and disappearing into the throng.

"Looks like your luck's finally run out," Breck said, swinging the muzzle of his crossbow between them. "You'd better come quietly."

"Actually, you're just in time," said Ruby. "We think the Oma Gang killed Alarick."

"Do we?" said Fillan.

"Sure they did," Breck replied. "And you're working for 'em."

"What?" said Ruby. "That's ridiculous."

Breck smirked, savouring his victory. "I suppose you stumbled into their top-secret gambling den accidentally."

"Of course not," said Ruby. "We came looking for clues."

"And just strolled in through the front door?" said Breck. "Gimme a break, kid. The NCPD has been staking out this joint for months. Two of our guys saw you arrive. Sloppy. Real sloppy."

"But it's the truth," said Fillan.

Breck gave a short, barking laugh. "What did they offer you to kill Alarick? It must have been a pretty sweet deal."

"Nobody offered us anything," said Ruby.

"Sweet enough for you to put your own coach in a coma when she got in your way."

His words goaded Ruby into sudden fury. "If you think I would ever do anything to hurt Marceline, then you're an even lousier detective than I thought!" She glared at him, nostrils flaring, but his smirk didn't waver.

"How about your friend here?" He prodded Fillan in the chest. "I hear you've been taking bites out of people."

Fillan shrank back, ears flat and tail limp.

"Yeah, that's what I thought," said Breck. "D'you know what happens to bite risks like you? They're not allowed out of their cells without a muzzle on."

Fillan cowered, his eyes wide. "Please, no!"

"You know he didn't attack Marceline," said Ruby. "It was the white wolf you shot at from the airship."

Breck's smirk disappeared abruptly. "I'm listening."

"His name's Hardulph," said Fillan. "He's a bounty hunter."

"Hunting who?"

"Us," said Ruby. "The Oma Gang must have hired him to track us down before we could solve the case."

"Before we could catch you and make you both blab, more like," said Breck. "They used you to kill Alarick, and now they're tidying up their loose ends."

Around them, the uniformed officers were marching casino patrons to the stairs, many of them still struggling and complaining. Their once fine evening wear was torn and bloodied, and some of them still clutched handfuls of betting chips.

"This is so stupid!" cried Ruby. "What do we have to do to convince you we're innocent?"

"I already told you, innocent people don't run," said Breck. "They don't break into apartments or flee the scene of an attempted murder, and they don't wind up in illegal gambling dens. So get moving." He grabbed them both by the arm and shoved them towards the stairs.

Ruby's stomach churned. This had been the most

important hunt of her life, and she had lost. Now she was going to lose everything else along with it – her friends, her career, her reputation. All she had to look forward to was a jail cell.

But she had barely set foot on the bottom step when she heard screaming and running from above. Breck pulled her back as police officers and casino patrons came pouring down from the Flower Haus.

"What's happening?" Breck demanded.

A guttural howl answered him from the top of the stairs, and Fillan slipped his paw into Ruby's hand.

"Hardulph," he said.

CHAPTER 24
Down and Out

The casino was in the grip of chaos once again, as police officers and patrons flooded back down the spiral stairs. Ruby saw Roselyn's parents among them, their faces pale and panic-stricken.

"What's going on?" demanded Breck.

"It's Hardulph," said Ruby, straining against his heavy grip on her arm.

Another furious howl made the air pulse. People screamed and whimpered. The officers all drew their crossbows and pointed them at the stairs.

"He only wants us," said Fillan. "But he'll hurt anyone who gets in his way."

Breck snapped a fresh gas canister into his crossbow. "I'd like to see him try. Get behind me."

"Breck's going to get us all killed," said Ruby as she and Fillan retreated to the centre of the casino. "We have to do something."

"I know, but what?"

She looked around. "There's no sign of Jarvin. Perhaps he had another way out of here."

Before they could act on the idea, however, heavy padding footsteps descended the stairs. Silence fell over the casino as, inch by sinewy inch, Hardulph stalked into view.

"NCPD!" shouted Breck. "Paws where we can see 'em!"

Hardulph regarded the row of police and bared his teeth in a horrible smile. The patrons crowded back as far as they could, and even some of the officers' hands trembled.

Ruby and Fillan stood their ground. The very sight of Hardulph filled Ruby with a disgust so deep and bitter that the feeling scared her a little. This was the creature that had almost killed Marceline.

"Hand over my prey," said Hardulph.

"Not gonna happen," Breck replied. "Come quietly, or we'll open fire."

Hardulph's grin widened. "At last, fair sport." He dropped to all fours, ready to spring.

"Do you have Jarvin's scent?" Ruby asked Fillan.

He sniffed. Nodded. "Those cigars of his really linger."

"Then I'm ready when you are," she replied.

Beyond the police line, Hardulph licked his maw. Then he took a step forward.

"Open fire!" yelled Breck.

A flurry of crossbow bolts filled the air, but struck harmlessly against the wall as Hardulph leaped clear. Before he hit the ground again, Fillan was on the move, down on all fours. Ruby ran with him.

The casino patrons panicked, scattering in all directions as they fought to get as far away from Hardulph as possible.

"This way," said Fillan, weaving between people's legs.

Behind them, Ruby heard Breck shouting to his officers. "Take him down!"

With a shout, the police charged. Ruby didn't look back, but heard the cacophony of breaking glass and splintering wood that followed. She stuck to Fillan's side as he cut across the room to the bar.

"Here," he said, climbing up and over it. "This is where his scent ends."

"But there's no exit here," she said, dropping down beside him. "He can't have just vanished."

Fillan sniffed quickly at the rows of bottles behind the

bar. "There was a hidden door upstairs," he said. "Maybe there's one down here too." He started lifting and twisting the bottles.

Ruby fought to keep her thoughts under control as Hardulph let out another gut-trembling howl.

"You can't hide from me," he roared. "I smell you!"

"Keep him back!" came an answering shout from Breck. "And someone call for backup!"

Ruby peeped over the bar. The casino was in complete disarray now, as patrons stampeded towards the stairs. Hardulph swept a couple of officers aside with one swipe of a paw, only for two more to jump him from behind.

A bottle smashed beside her, showering her with a pungent blue liquid.

"Sorry!" Fillan looked abashed. "It slipped."

It was as she ducked below the bar again that she saw it – the liquor was draining away through a strangely shaped crack in the floorboards. It was a perfect right angle. "Here." Being careful of the broken glass, she groped along the crack until she felt something. A catch, set into the floor. She pulled it, and a square section of the boards popped open.

"A trapdoor!" said Fillan.

They peered into the opening. A rickety old ladder disappeared into darkness below.

"What if Jarvin's waiting down there for us?" asked Fillan.

"He's got to be better than what's waiting for us up here," she replied. And without another word, she swung her legs into the hole.

They hadn't descended far when Ruby began to have second thoughts. They only deepened when Fillan pulled the hatch shut after them, plunging them both into total darkness. At least, total darkness for her.

"It's not far to the bottom," Fillan told her. "Take it steady."

"I forgot that wolves can see better in the dark," she said, fumbling her way down the cold, pitted rungs.

A few moments later their feet touched solid ground and, as her eyes adjusted, Ruby was able to make out a low-ceilinged chamber of rough stone, with several openings leading away into deeper, thicker darkness. "Where are we?"

"An old sewer, maybe," Fillan replied. "The Oma Gang must use it to move around the city without attracting attention."

"Which way did Jarvin go?"

Fillan sniffed, and pointed at one of the openings.

"Follow me." He led her at a swift trot along the tunnel. The air was cold and damp, and Ruby felt strands of cobweb brush against her face.

"I've been thinking," said Fillan. "What if the Oma Gang loaned Alarick the money to build the training centre?"

It was such a simple idea, and the moment it entered Ruby's mind, several other pieces of the puzzle clicked into place around it. "Of course!" she said. "If he couldn't find a bank willing to give him the money, he'd have had to turn to someone like the Oma Gang. They're loan sharks."

"That explains what 'Pay your dues' meant," said Fillan. "He must have fallen behind on his payments, so they took their revenge."

She remembered the look of defeat on Alarick's face as he read the note. Perhaps he'd known what was coming, although he couldn't have guessed he'd already inhaled the poison that would end his life. With a cold start, she realized he had doomed himself, right in front of her, and none of them had known it.

A curious leaden sensation welled up deep in her bones, spreading out until it became an ache that occupied her entire body. It was grief, she realized. For Alarick.

"He was trying to do something good, and they killed

him so they could make their money back when the match was voided," she said. "We can't let them get away with it."

"Agreed."

They ran in silence for a while. A very long while, Ruby thought. Ten minutes after leaving the casino, they were still going, pausing now and then at forks in the passageway so Fillan could recapture Jarvin's scent. *Where on earth do all these tunnels lead?* she wondered. Nevertheless, it didn't feel as though they had gone far enough when the sound of heavy footsteps echoed from behind them. Ruby gripped Fillan's shoulder tightly.

"Maybe it's Breck and the police," he said.

"You know it's not," she replied.

Sure enough, when Hardulph's howl came, the confines of the tunnels amplified and distorted it into a horrifying scream.

"Faster!" said Ruby.

They broke into a sprint so fast that Ruby's legs burned, despite all her training. Fillan panted and yelped beside her, stumbling with every other step. Then he fell and, for a horrifying second, she couldn't find him in the dark.

"I smell you!" came Hardulph's voice, booming from all around them.

"Fillan?" Her voice was shrill with panic.

"Go," he answered. "I can't keep running."

She zeroed in on his voice and reached out until she found his paws. "Yes, you can."

"But..."

"But nothing," she snapped. "There's a hunter coming. What do you do?"

"I don't know."

"Yes, you do. Now say it."

He squeezed her hand tightly. "I run."

"So do it!"

They floundered on, Ruby's skin crawling at the thought of Hardulph close behind them. Any second now, she might feel his teeth closing on her.

Just as panic started to tighten her airway, the floor sloped sharply upward and a breath of fresh night air brushed her face.

"I smell Wild Wood Roses!" said Fillan.

A second later they were outside, surrounded by the brooding shapes of tall trees. Moonlight filtered down through a thick canopy of branches.

"I don't believe it," said Ruby. "We're in the Wild Wood."

And there, across a small clearing carpeted with pine needles, was a log cabin, its shutters brightly painted and its roof shaggy with moss. A lantern burned on the porch, attracting moths.

"There you both are," said a woman's voice.

The lantern illuminated an old lady in a rocking chair. She was small, with grey curls and an old-fashioned dress. A woollen blanket was draped over her knees, on which sat a pile of knitting.

Ruby and Fillan were so startled that they froze, until the woman pointed past them.

"Well? Hurry up. I'm expecting more company."

They crossed the clearing at a run and made it to the porch as Hardulph emerged from the tunnel. His eyes glinted red in the moonlight.

"No more running," he said. "It ends here."

Ruby shuddered. "You hurt Marceline!"

"I hurt lots of people," Hardulph replied. "But give yourselves up and I'll make this painless."

He started towards the cottage, but the old woman raised a hand.

"No, I don't think so." There was an edge of steel in her voice that was enough to make him pause.

"I don't take orders from you, old woman."

"The name's Orlantha," she replied. "And you'd better start taking orders, because as long as these two are on my property, *I'll* decide what happens to them."

Fillan and Ruby looked at each other in amazement.

"Be careful," said Ruby. "He's dangerous."

"Oh, I know, dear," said Orlantha. "But do you know

what's more dangerous than him?"

"What?"

Orlantha smiled. "Me." She clicked her fingers, and something erupted from the ground beneath Hardulph's feet. Dirt and pine needles flew everywhere, forcing Ruby to shield her face. When she looked again, Hardulph was struggling in a net, suspended several metres above the clearing from a tree branch. He snapped and clawed at the thick ropes, but only succeeded in making the net spin uncontrollably.

Orlantha clapped her hands demurely. Ruby and Fillan looked at one another in disbelief.

"How was that, Oma?" Jarvin emerged from the trees, followed by three large, tattooed men bearing crossbows.

"Perfect timing, dear."

It took a few seconds for Ruby to process what she'd just heard, and the realization formed a cold, hard lump in the pit of her stomach. "He called you Oma."

"It means *grandmother* in the old tongue," Orlantha replied. "Jarvin here is my second daughter's eldest. And he's a good boy." She reached up and ruffled Jarvin's hair as he joined them on the porch. The other men stood guard around the net.

Ruby took an involuntary step back. "So the Oma Gang…"

"Is my operation, yes. And a very successful one, until you two ruined everything." She pulled the blanket off her legs to reveal a harpoon gun, which she pointed right between Ruby's eyes. "Hands up, please, dears."

CHAPTER 25
The Cabin in the Woods

Ruby and Fillan kept their hands in the air as Orlantha marched them at harpoon-point into the cottage. It was a cosy space, with china ducks on the wall, a great many bookcases, and a brass kettle whistling over a roaring fireplace. Certainly not what Ruby would have pictured as the lair of a criminal mastermind.

Jarvin followed them in, leaving his men to guard Hardulph in the net outside. He took the kettle off the heat and filled a teapot on a small trolley.

"Take a seat." Orlantha gestured to an overstuffed tartan sofa and settled in a matching armchair opposite. She winced as her knees popped, but the barbed tip of the harpoon gun never wavered. "You two have caused me a great deal of trouble," she said. "I expect an apology and an explanation, or I'll skewer you both to a tree and leave your bodies for the wolves. Macaroon?" She nodded to a biscuit tin beside the teapot. Ruby, who couldn't take her eyes off the wicked tip of the harpoon, shook her head.

Her mind swam as she realized the magnitude of her mistake. She had been so desperate to track down Alarick's killer that she had ignored Fillan's plea to fetch help from Charlotte. Now she had landed them both in even greater danger than before.

"Start talkin'," said Jarvin, filling a teacup and setting it on the arm of Orlantha's chair.

"We had no idea the police were watching your casino," said Fillan. "We didn't even know it *was* a casino until we got inside."

"I don't care about the casino," said Orlantha. "I'm talking about Alarick. He was about to make me a fortune when you killed him."

Ruby looked at Fillan, and then back at Orlantha. "We didn't kill him," she said. "You did."

"I did nothing of the sort."

Ruby shook her head in an effort to clear her confusion. "But you sent him the roses. And the note. 'Pay your dues'?"

"How exactly is he supposed to pay me anything if he's dead?"

"Through your betting ring," said Fillan. "You got to keep half of everyone's money."

Orlantha chuckled. "You think I'd kill Alarick for *half* a fortune? He owed me a whole one, with interest."

"So you *did* lend him the money to build the training centre!" said Ruby.

Orlantha raised her teacup and took a sip. "A significant investment, but a very profitable one. Alarick would have been paying me back for the rest of his life, and with the interest rates I was charging him, I'd have tripled my money."

"That sounds like a terrible deal for him," said Ruby.

"The guy was desperate," said Jarvin. "Said this training centre had to happen at any cost. And the banks wouldn't lend him squat."

"Because he was so bad with money," said Fillan.

Orlantha sighed and replaced her cup. "I hadn't realized quite *how* bad until he missed his first three payments."

Ruby fought to process all this, but it was difficult to concentrate with the tip of the harpoon still aimed at her forehead. "You *must* have killed him," she said. "It's the only thing that makes sense."

"Actually, I'm not sure it does," said Fillan. "Think about it. She obviously isn't working with Hardulph."

"The white wolf outside?" said Orlantha. "He's nothing to do with me."

"You see?" said Fillan. "We assumed the Oma Gang killed Alarick for the betting money, and then hired Hardulph to hunt us down before we could expose the truth. But if Hardulph isn't working for them, then they're probably telling the truth about Alarick as well."

"But what about the bouquet?" said Ruby. "And the note?"

"The roses weren't poisoned when they left the Flower Haus," said Orlantha. "Someone must have interfered with them before they reached Alarick. The note was just a little encouragement before the game, in case he got cold feet."

Ruby frowned. "Encouragement for what?"

Orlantha paused to accept a macaroon from Jarvin, served on a plate with a doily. "He was going to repay some of his debt by losing the Tooth and Claw final."

Ruby's mouth went dry. "Impossible."

"Hardly," said Orlantha. "My betting ring took millions of florins on yesterday's game, and Alarick's been the favourite to win all season. Imagine the upset if he lost."

Fillan's ears twitched. "You'd keep all those failed bets."

"Precisely. A far larger sum than simply keeping half

of everything. Alarick agreed to battle bravely through to the last points, and then let this young lady slip past him to win. He thought it would look dramatic."

All eyes turned to Ruby, but she was too sickened to respond. The cosy warmth of the cottage was suddenly cloying and claustrophobic. Sweat broke out on her face, and her breath was caught in her throat. She remembered Alarick's look of defeat in the Hunter's Den as he read the note, and his words to her in the arena. *I saved you until last…*

"Alarick hated the idea, of course," said Orlantha. "He still had his pride, but it seems he valued the training centre more."

Ruby slumped back against the sofa, winded. She didn't know about Alarick's pride, but she felt her own wither up and die. It had all been fake. The victory she had trained so hard for, that she had been within seconds of claiming, had been a sham. Alarick hadn't even been trying to catch her.

Dimly, as if from a great distance, she heard Fillan speak.

"If you didn't kill him, and neither did we, then this has all been a huge misunderstanding."

"So it would seem," said Orlantha.

"Which means you can let us go."

Orlantha gave him a quizzical look over the rim of her teacup. Jarvin laughed.

"What's so funny?" said Fillan.

"The idea that we're gonna let you walk," said Jarvin.

"I'm afraid he's right," said Orlantha. "You've seen my face, for one thing. You've found my smuggling tunnels and my cottage, and I've explained my match-fixing scheme to you. You're not leaving here alive."

Fillan took Ruby's hand and squeezed it hard. Ruby knew she should be terrified, but she was just numb. How could she feel anything after what she'd just been told?

"That wolf outside wants to make a meal of you both," said Orlantha. "I don't see why he should go hungry. Jarvin, be a dear and untie him, will you? His dinner will be served momentarily."

"Sure thing, Oma."

He let himself out, and Orlantha levered herself to her feet. "Of course, I'll have to put an end to the wolf as well when he's finished with you, but that can't be helped."

Fillan was gripping Ruby's hand so tightly now that she winced.

"You don't have to do this," he said. "We promise not to tell a soul!"

Orlantha gave him a pitying smile. "It's nothing personal, my dear. In fact, I'll send a bouquet of Wild

Wood Roses to each of your families. Anonymously, of course. Now, shall we get it over with?" She gestured with the harpoon gun.

Ruby stood. "It's not fair."

"I know," said Orlantha. "But that's never stopped me before."

"Not this," said Ruby. "I'm talking about the last year of my life. All the time and effort I sacrificed to beat Alarick. And now you tell me it was all for nothing."

Orlantha tutted. "Oh dear. As last words go, those weren't the best." With another prompt from the harpoon gun, she ushered them outside.

CHAPTER 26
Catch and Release

The lantern still burned on the porch as Ruby stepped outside, seething with anger and dismay. The Tooth & Claw final was supposed to have been her ultimate test, but now she knew the whole thing had been a fix. Alarick would have let her win, whatever happened.

And I'll never find out who killed him, she thought bitterly.

Her earlier sorrow at his death had vanished. Now she wished he was still alive so she could throttle him.

Fillan followed, still gripping her hand and trembling with fear. When they saw what lay before them, however, they both stopped abruptly.

"There's no use delaying the inevitable," said Orlantha in the doorway behind them. "Hurry up, please."

They stepped aside, revealing the scene. The net that had held Hardulph lay in tatters across the clearing, and there was no sign of Jarvin or the guards, although a few broken crossbows lay among the pine needles.

Orlantha's demeanour hardened in an instant. "Jarvin?"

No answer came. Even the background clicks and chirrups of the moonlit forest had fallen silent. The Wild Wood held its breath.

"Maybe we should go back inside," said Fillan.

"Wait." Orlantha pointed to two small dark shapes on the ground not far from the porch. "Jarvin's boots. Why would he leave those behind?" She jabbed Fillan in the back with the harpoon, until he grudgingly stepped off the porch and approached them.

He picked up one of the boots, sniffed it, looked inside, and dropped it immediately. "Because his feet are still inside them." He reeled back to the protection of the porch, but Orlantha levelled the harpoon at him. Her hands, previously steady, now trembled.

"You're lying," she said.

He shrank from the weapon's wavering tip. "I wish I was."

For an awful moment, Ruby thought Orlantha was going to shoot him. Instead, all the colour drained from the old woman's face.

"My boy…" she gasped, and let the weapon hang limp at her side.

Ruby took a tentative step towards her. "I'm sorry," she said. "But Hardulph's going to do the same to all of us if we don't get out of here."

Orlantha stared vacantly at her for a moment. Then she blinked, and the ruthless glint was back in her eyes.

"Not all of us," she said, raising the harpoon gun again. "Just you."

A low, gurgling laugh seeped out of the darkness between the trees. "The old woman is right," came Hardulph's voice. "I only want my prey."

Ruby cried out as Orlantha grabbed her arm and shoved her off the porch beside Fillan.

"Here they are!" Orlantha cried. "Show yourself!" Her gaze was as hard as flint, scanning the treeline for any sign of movement. Ruby dropped into a crouch and did the same.

"Anything?" she whispered to Fillan. He sniffed the air.

"There's too much background scent from the Wild Wood Roses. He's hard to pin down."

When Hardulph spoke again, his voice came from the opposite side of the clearing. "Trying to lure me out to shoot me, old woman? Go back inside, and count yourself lucky that you're too feeble for me to bother with."

Orlantha pouted, pivoted, and fired the harpoon at the patch of darkness from which Hardulph's voice had come. It streaked into the void and vanished without a sound. "Feeble, am I?"

"And slow." Hardulph strolled out of the treeline on his hind legs, twirling the harpoon like a baton between the claws of one paw.

Ruby and Fillan backed away. Orlantha didn't even notice – she held her head high and hissed with anger. "You'd better kill me now, because I warn you, if you don't, I'll hunt you to the ends of the earth for what you've done."

Hardulph approached until he was paws to toes with her, then tapped her on the nose with the tip of the harpoon. Orlantha, to her credit, didn't even blink.

"I would enjoy that hunt," he said. "So make your choice – stay and die, or go inside and live."

Orlantha's face was a mask of fury, but she backed onto the porch and cast the harpoon gun on the ground.

"You're giving up?" cried Ruby.

"Merely cutting my losses," Orlantha replied. "I can't plot my revenge if I'm dead, now can I?" With a last, defiant look at Hardulph, she slipped into the cottage and slammed the door.

Hardulph turned his hungry grin on Ruby and Fillan, who stumbled backwards across the clearing. "Run," he said. "It's no sport otherwise."

Fillan turned to flee, but Ruby yanked him back to her side. "Not yet," she whispered. "We split up. He can't follow us both."

"He'll just chase me down and then go after you."

"Not if I make sure he comes for me first." She reached into her top and tore the bandage off the shoulder wound that Hardulph had inflicted on her in the paper mill. "I bet you can't resist the scent of blood, can you, Hardulph?"

Sure enough, Hardulph's nostrils flared and his fur bristled from head to foot. "Run," he repeated.

Ruby took Charlotte's business card from her pocket and pressed it into Fillan's hands. "Go back through the tunnels, find Charlotte and tell her everything we've learned. I'll meet you both later." She knew that wolves couldn't go pale, but she was pretty sure that Fillan would have, had he been able.

"You don't have to do this," he said.

"Yes, I do."

She shoved him away and he stumbled towards the trees. Hardulph started after him, until Ruby tossed the bloody bandage at his feet.

"You want a real hunt?" she said. "I'll give you one."

"Yesssss." Hardulph broke off his pursuit and circled her. "The wolf and the girl in the woods. The way it always was."

"So you accept?"

He lowered his great head until it was level with hers. "Start running. Fear makes your flesh taste sweeter."

She stared into his maw and tried not to flinch. "Oh, I'll run all right. It's what I'm trained for. But on one condition."

Hardulph straightened. "No conditions! Run or fall, live or die. Those are the only rules of the hunt."

"And if you want to hunt me, I'm adding one more," said Ruby. "If I make it back to Netherburg, you let me and Fillan go. And you give me a prize for winning."

She fought to keep her rising terror in check as Hardulph continued to circle her.

"What prize?"

"I don't know yet," she replied. "I'll decide when I win."

He laughed. "If you win, you live. That's the prize."

Ruby swallowed and mustered her courage. She had hoped it wouldn't come to this. "Fine," she said. "Kill me here." So saying, she sat down cross-legged and closed her eyes. "You wouldn't have beaten me anyway."

She laced her fingers together to stop her hands from shaking, and listened to the soft padding of Hardulph's footsteps. Would he strike? Or was he so driven by the thrill of the hunt that he was willing to risk letting her go?

"Very well," he said. "I accept. Now run."

Ruby sprang to her feet, every nerve alert. "How much head start do I have?"

Hardulph licked his maw. "Ten."

Ruby raised both eyebrows. "Ten minutes? That's a lot."

"Nine," said Hardulph. "Eight. Seven…"

She turned and fled, her blood pumping in her ears. This was it. No tricks, no lies, no schemes – her real test. Hardulph's howl echoed through the night as the Wild Wood closed in around her.

CHAPTER 27
Pursuit

The Wild Wood wasn't like the Tooth & Claw arena. Ruby was used to trimmed grass, crash mats and balance beams. Not pitted earth, tree roots that threatened to twist her ankle at every step, and dense undergrowth that whipped and cut at her exposed skin.

She didn't dare slow, however. Hardulph was behind her and closing fast, his heavy footsteps approaching through the dark. So she ran headlong between trees that loomed over her like the columns of some great, dark cathedral. It must be nearly dawn, she thought, but the light was locked away behind the whispering canopy overhead. The forest resented the daylight, and guarded the darkness jealously.

Puffing hard, she crested a small rise and half ran, half

fell down the other side, landing on her hands and knees in a shallow stream. *Follow the stream*, she thought. *Keep my scent out of Hardulph's nose.*

She stumbled along the stony bed, her shoes flooding with cold water. But the stream was leading her at an angle away from Netherburg, she realized. She couldn't follow it much longer if she wanted to stay ahead of Hardulph.

A horrible realization struck her with such force that she almost stopped. She couldn't outrun him. The terrain was too difficult, and he was too fast. If she continued to run, she was finished.

But what if she didn't need to run?

She pushed her fear to one side and cleared her mind. She couldn't keep following the stream, and if she left it in the direction of Netherburg, Hardulph would catch her in moments.

But only because she'd been thinking like prey – fleeing from danger and towards safety. How often did Hardulph's prey do the opposite? With renewed purpose, she climbed out of the stream and turned back towards Orlantha's cottage.

She had to find a way past Hardulph, a way to get behind him. After a few metres, she found what she needed – a thick bush of Wild Wood Roses twined around

213

the base of a tree. The flowers had interfered with Fillan's nose; maybe they'd do the same to Hardulph's. Ruby dropped to all fours and crawled in between the thorny stems. Then she waited, and watched.

She didn't have to wait long. There was the barest whisper among the undergrowth, then the gaunt white shape of Hardulph appeared, nose to the ground, sniffing back and forth along the near bank of the stream. He paused at the spot at which Ruby had emerged from the water.

"You're here," he growled. "No use hiding."

Ruby's heart stuttered in her chest, but she held her nerve, and her breath. *If he really knew where I was, I'd be dead already*, she told herself.

Nevertheless, she screwed her eyes shut when Hardulph reared his head in her direction. There was a moment of dreadful silence, during which she expected the sharp pain of his teeth at any second. When nothing happened, she opened her eyes again. Hardulph had vanished.

Her relief was short-lived. Where was he? Had he crossed the stream towards Netherburg? Or was he lurking, waiting for her to make the next move?

She huddled in the dirt, breathing slowly and shallowly so as to make as little noise as possible. Her legs burned with cramp and her bottom went numb, but still she didn't move. If Hardulph was waiting, she would wait longer.

There was a rustle close by, and the bush in which she sat trembled as something brushed past it. She looked up through the roses, saw white fur a few centimetres from her face, and swallowed the scream that tried to force its way up her throat. Hardulph was standing over her. The hunt was over.

"I said stop hiding!" he roared. His voice shook petals from the rose bush, but it gave Ruby sudden hope. He hadn't seen her. More importantly, he hadn't smelled her either! He turned in circles, watching the forest for movement, his tail swishing impatiently.

"Tricked me," he said to himself. "Sneaky girl."

With another deafening howl, he bounded away, leaping the stream in a single step. Within seconds, he was just a dim shape receding into the shadows.

Ruby finally let her breath out, and slumped against the tree. It had worked. Hardulph had caught up, but she had slipped through his clutches. Now he assumed that she was several minutes ahead of him, but he had no scent to follow, and no trail to pursue. His instincts were of no use to him any more, and that gave her the advantage.

Moving slowly, so as not to make any noise, she crept out from the bush, forded the stream, and set off in pursuit.

CHAPTER 28
Gatekeeper

The closer Ruby got to the edge of the Wild Wood, the thinner the undergrowth became. That meant less cover to hide in, but it also meant that narrow trails opened up between the trees, and she was able to make more progress.

Nevertheless, she kept low to the ground and moved as carefully as she could. Hardulph was somewhere between her and Netherburg, and she didn't want to lose the element of surprise by running into him unexpectedly.

One by one the trails converged, until they formed a trodden path that wound between the great trunks. The forest canopy thinned, allowing the first glimmers of dawn to shine through – milky blue, fading to pink on the horizon.

At last Ruby reached the edge of the forest. The trees petered out into open meadowland, dotted with wild flowers. The path stretched across it, becoming more defined until it reached the city's old stone defensive wall, where it passed beneath the Wolf Gate.

This was the boundary between the Wild Wood and human territory, and several officers manned the gate's checkpoint. They all kept a steady eye on Hardulph, who stalked back and forth across the meadow, watching the woods.

He's figured out that I wasn't ahead of him, Ruby thought. *He's waiting for me to show up.*

And she would have to show up, she realized. Though she sat and thought about it for five long, agonizing minutes, she knew there was no other way. Trickery had got her to within sight of her goal, but now she had no choice but to face Hardulph one on one. They were into the endgame and this was the winning point.

She emerged onto the path and shook the dewdrops from her clothes. "Hello, Hardulph."

He grinned horribly. "At last. Not a runner but a hider."

"A survivor." She jogged on the spot and waved in greeting to the border guards, who were now all pointing at her in frantic recognition. "Are you ready?"

Hardulph planted his hind paws in the dust of the path. The officers behind him drew their crossbows, and one of them ran to the security kiosk in the middle of the gateway and picked up the phone. Calling in reinforcements, no doubt.

"I've decided on my prize," she said.

Hardulph laughed. "Name it."

"If I make it through the gate, you tell me who hired you."

He cocked his head to one side, then the other. "Nothing more?"

"That's all."

"Deal," he said. "Now stop stalling for time and—"

Ruby was already running, full tilt, straight towards him. She didn't veer left or right, she just charged, as if she could knock him down like a bowling pin. Hardulph looked startled, then delighted. He bared his teeth, planted his feet wide, and prepared to catch her.

When she had closed half the distance, Ruby shot a glance at the space between his legs. Hardulph caught the look and dropped his paws to block her. His grin widened.

So did Ruby's, because now she knew he was following her lead. With only metres to spare, she twisted her body to the right. Hardulph leaped, his great paws reaching for her.

Ruby pirouetted, ducked, and threw herself between the grasping paws. Now that he had raised them, she had space to roll through his legs, and she sprang back to her feet behind him. She heard his furious howl as she ran, jumped, and landed in the waiting grasp of the officers inside the gateway.

"Ruby Calvino?" one of them said. "You're nicked."

"Nooooooo!" With a cry, Hardulph rushed at them, only to skid to a halt as the officers raised their crossbows.

"Back away!" one of them shouted.

Hardulph stood, panting, on the city's threshold. "Impossible!" he shouted. "I have never lost a hunt."

"You lost this one," said Ruby. "So hold up your end of the deal. Who hired you?"

He glared at her, saliva falling in strings from his mouth and pattering on the soil.

"Back to the Wild Wood with you," said one of the officers. "This girl is under our jurisdiction."

Ruby fought against the officer as he tried to pull her away. "Tell me!" she shouted. "Who hired you? Is it Roselyn? Her parents?"

Hardulph's eyes blazed. "Grimm," he said. "She calls herself Charlotte Grimm."

Ruby went limp in the officer's grasp. "Charlotte?"

A second officer caught her under the arms and the

two men dragged her away from the checkpoint, into the city.

"Half of Netherburg's been looking for you," the first officer said. "I reckon we'll get a juicy little promotion once we hand you over to Detective Breck. Whaddaya think, Hank?"

"Yeah," said the second guard. "And maybe a medal from the mayor."

Ruby barely listened – her mind was too full of Charlotte Grimm. She didn't want to believe Hardulph, but her instincts told her he wasn't a liar. If Charlotte had hired him, then she must have killed Alarick. But why? What did she have to gain from his death? Ruby tried to make the idea fit with everything else she and Fillan had learned, but couldn't. Had they overlooked something?

The thought of Fillan brought her back to herself with a start. "Please," she said. "Lock me up if you want, but you have to send officers to find Charlotte Grimm. She's a reporter with the *Netherburg Gazette*. I sent my friend Fillan to her, but she's dangerous. She murdered Alarick."

Both men laughed. "Nice try," said the first officer.

"I'm telling the truth!" she said. "She hired that wolf out there to kill me. You heard him say it!"

"Whoever that wolf was, you don't have to worry about

him any more," said Hank. "Breck'll be here to collect you soon."

Then the screaming started. Ruby looked over her shoulder in time to see Hardulph sweep aside the two officers still guarding the checkpoint with a mighty blow. His way clear, he bounded after her.

"I will not be humiliated!" he roared.

Her captors released their hold on her, turned, and opened fire. Crossbow bolts cracked and pinged off the nearby house fronts, and Hardulph twisted in mid-air to avoid them, falling a few metres short of Ruby.

The two guards in the gateway recovered themselves and charged Hardulph from behind with their batons.

Ruby didn't wait to see what happened – she turned and ran. She was tired, but knew she couldn't slow. Death was on her heels again and, somewhere in the dense and noisy city that lay before her, was Charlotte Grimm. A new hunt had begun.

CHAPTER 29
Bad Press

People stared at Ruby as she sprinted through Netherburg. The city rose early, and the streets were already busy, especially here in the east side, where the markets and industrial sectors never really slept. People clearly recognized her – she could see it in their faces. It didn't help that her own face looked down from a thousand wanted posters, plastered to every street lamp, postbox and shopfront.

Let them stare. Let them call the police. She had something more important to worry about – she had sent Fillan into danger.

Find Charlotte Grimm, she had told him. Charlotte, who was supposed to be on their side. Charlotte, the keeper of Marceline's and Alarick's secrets. Charlotte, the traitor.

If she wants me and Fillan dead, why didn't she kill us both in the diner last night? she wondered as she skidded around a corner, dodging the first commuter tram of the day. *Why help us instead? We wouldn't have found the Flower Haus without her.*

Something about this still didn't add up, but the answers could wait. Right now, Fillan needed her.

If he had called Charlotte, she would have wanted to hide him away somewhere quiet. Somewhere they wouldn't be seen. Somewhere…abandoned?

She turned east, and ran harder.

It took her thirty minutes to reach the paper mill, by which time her stamina was waning. Panting hard, she took shelter behind a lean-to shed across the small square from the mill's entrance, but there was nothing much to see. Ribbons of police tape decorated the gates, beyond which she could just make out a few uniformed officers loitering in the old lumber yard. With a bitter start, Ruby realized that, once again, she hadn't thought things through. The mill was a crime scene now – of course the police would still be here. Which meant that Charlotte and Fillan definitely *weren't*.

Looking around again, she saw something that gave

her hope. A small group of reporters milled about in the square, away from the gates. She recognized a few of them from the crowd outside the hospital as she approached.

"Hi," she said. "I'm looking for Charlotte Grimm."

The reaction was immediate. The group pressed around her, every reporter barking questions, while microphones and cameras were shoved in her face.

"Are you working with the Oma Gang?"

"Are you here to hand yourself in?"

"Do you think you'll kill again?"

Ruby rolled her eyes and signalled for quiet. "I'm innocent and I can prove it. But I need to find Charlotte. It's a matter of life and death."

A man with a white handlebar moustache and chequered jacket spoke up. "Hans Zimmerman, *Netherburg Gazette* crime desk. She left the newsroom at a run this morning, said she was heading for the stadium. No idea why. No stories there any more. Place is virtually deserted." His moustache twitched. "You haven't signed for an exclusive with her, have you? An interview with Alarick's killer would be one heck of a scoop. How about it?"

Ruby held up a finger, calling for a pause. She should have thought to check the stadium – as a sports reporter, Charlotte could pretty much come and go from it as she pleased. There was even a dedicated press entrance…

That thought gave her the beginnings of an idea. "Hans, I'll give you the whole story if you can get me to the stadium without being seen."

Hans wavered, clearly enticed but cautious too. "I don't know," he said. "Aiding and abetting a criminal, and all that."

"I'm not a criminal," she replied. "And by the end of this you'll have the scoop of the century."

"Hey, what about us?" said one of the other reporters. There was a grumbling chorus of agreement from his fellows.

"You can all come," she said. "This story's big enough to share."

The reporters looked at one another in silence before Hans puffed his chest out. "We're in," he said.

Netherburg Stadium was indeed virtually deserted. With no matches on, the building was staffed by a handful of cleaners and attendants, so Ruby didn't encounter anyone as she padded through the subterranean utility areas. It felt eerie, but it was a relief to be out of Hans Zimmerman's car; she'd spent the last twenty minutes curled up out of sight in the passenger footwell, relating her and Fillan's experiences as Hans and the other reporters drove in convoy to the stadium. She wasn't sure how much of it Hans actually *believed* yet, but he'd stuck to his end of the bargain and now here she was. The security guard on duty at the stadium's press entrance had barely glanced up from his crossword as the group arrived, with Ruby hidden among them in a borrowed coat.

"Call the police," she told Hans, once they'd all reached the relative safety of the press room, no Charlotte or Fillan in sight. "Tell them where we are and what's happening. Then I need you all in position for Phase Two."

"Which is?" asked Hans.

"You'll know it when it happens," she replied.

She watched them all scurry away, and steeled herself for what she knew was going to be the hard part. She had a plan, but if even one part of it went wrong, the results could be fatal, for her and for Fillan.

"Fillan?" she called, stepping into the corridor. "Charlotte?"

There was no answer. Swiftly and silently, she moved through the empty passages until she detected the faint sound of voices. They were coming from the direction of the Runners' locker room and, as she crept closer, she realized that one of the voices belonged to Fillan. He sounded scared.

"Even if you do this, how will it help?" he said.

"Shut up!" Charlotte snapped in response. "I'm trying to think."

Ruby threw the door open. "About what?"

She took a quiet satisfaction from Charlotte's look of horror. The reporter stood over Fillan, a crossbow in one hand and a framed picture in the other. Ruby recognized it as one of the team portraits from the walls.

"Ruby, run!" cried Fillan. "She killed Alarick!"

"I know," said Ruby, letting the door swing shut behind her. "Hardulph told me."

"Impossible," said Charlotte. "He works for me."

"Not any more."

Ruby was trying to act casual, but she had never felt so focused in her life. "Let him go."

Charlotte waved the crossbow in Fillan's face. "And give up my only leverage?"

"The police are coming," said Ruby.

"Coming for you," said Charlotte. "They've got no evidence against me. No motive."

Ruby hesitated. "Maybe not. But don't you think they'll be suspicious when they see you waving a weapon around?"

"That's easy," said Charlotte. "After the attack on Marceline, I was scared for my safety, so I bought a sidearm. And just as well, because Alarick's killers cornered me here in the stadium, and I had to shoot them both in self-defence."

Fillan turned his terrified gaze on Ruby. "What do we do?"

Ruby levelled a look at Charlotte. "Why did you kill Alarick?"

"Because he was a wild animal," Charlotte replied. "And when animals hurt people, they deserve to be put down."

Ruby frowned. "You killed him to avenge Marceline?"

"Not Marceline." Charlotte's face crumpled into an ugly mask of fury. "Me! I did it for me, and the person I could have been if he hadn't…" She caught herself, took a deep breath, and continued. "I was a good player. The Riverside Runners were going places, climbing up the league table. I thought I might be the next big thing, until Alarick happened."

"He hurt you?" asked Ruby.

"He didn't have to," Charlotte replied. "It started with threats on the pitch. Then menacing notes in my locker. Scratch marks on my apartment door when I got home. Raw meat in my mailbox."

Fillan flattened his ears to his skull. "That's… horrible!"

Charlotte nodded. "I tried toughing it out, but I'd stopped sleeping. I was scared to go to team practices, or be alone after dark. I had nightmares about what might happen the next time we had to play him. When he put Marceline out of action, I took it as a final warning. So I quit the sport."

Ruby let her arms drop to her sides. "Oh, Charlotte, I'm so sorry. I had no idea."

"Of course you didn't. Because nobody remembers." Charlotte turned the team photograph out to face Ruby. "I'm just another face on the wall. Hundreds of people walk past this photo every week, but when was the last time anyone actually looked at it? Did you?"

Ruby looked away, but not before she had seen the smiling blond girl at the far left of the portrait. She had Charlotte's face, but with none of the cares or fears etched into it. She couldn't have been much older than Akako.

"Not even Alarick remembered," Charlotte continued. "He bullied lots of us out of the sport. We were all just steps on his path to stardom, and once he'd ground us underfoot, he moved on."

"What about Marceline?" said Ruby. "Did she know?"

Charlotte nodded. "It's why we became friends. He'd ruined both our lives and we hated him. Until she decided that didn't matter."

"You mean when she forgave him," said Ruby.

Charlotte snapped the crossbow around to point at her. "She turned her back on everything we'd been through. Alarick stole our futures, and then came crawling back to her. And she accepted him!" Charlotte's face glowed purple. "How dare they!" She hurled the portrait to the floor, scattering glass shards in all directions.

"It isn't fair," said Ruby. "And I'm sorry for you. But what you're doing now isn't fair either. This isn't Fillan's fault, or mine. Please, just let us go."

Charlotte shook her head. "I wish I could, but it's too late for that."

"Is it?" said Fillan. "You could have killed us at my parents' diner last night, or set Hardulph on us. But you helped us instead."

"Good point," said Ruby.

"I helped you to help myself," Charlotte replied. "I panicked when I got your note, but I played along to find out how much you knew, and how much trouble you were going to be. And the answer was *lots* of trouble. I had no idea where Hardulph was though, so I had to improvise. Taking you to the Flower Haus seemed like the ideal solution – I may be a sports journalist, but you don't spend half your life in a newsroom in this city without learning a thing or two about the Oma Gang. I knew they ran the place, and I figured that you two would last about ten seconds once you walked in and started asking questions."

A chill crept through Ruby's bones. "You were going to let them kill us for you?"

"Exactly," Charlotte replied. "If I get rid of you two, this all goes away." She grabbed Fillan by the scruff of the neck. "Who wants to go first?"

"Ruby?" said Fillan. "Help!"

Ruby raised her hands in a calming gesture, although they shook with nerves. "It'll be okay," she told him. "Remember you're a vegetarian."

"W-what?"

"Except when you're not." She winked.

He looked blank for a moment, before a spark of understanding lit in his eyes. With a mighty effort, he twisted in Charlotte's grip and sank his teeth deep into the hand holding the crossbow. She screamed, dropped the weapon, and then dropped Fillan.

"Run!" said Ruby.

He leaped to her side, and they burst out of the locker room together into the corridor.

"I can't believe you beat Hardulph," he panted as they ran up the players' tunnel.

"I almost didn't," she replied.

A crossbow bolt whistled past her ear, and she looked

back to see Charlotte, red-faced and dripping blood from her hand, in pursuit.

"Keep going," said Ruby. "We're nearly there."

"Where?" said Fillan.

"The end of all this. Follow me."

They emerged from the tunnel into the startling daylight of the arena. It felt so strange to be back again. The obstacles and cut-out trees from yesterday's final were all still in place, but the stadium felt strangely funereal without the whisper and roar of the crowd.

"Just up ahead," said Ruby, leading Fillan towards the treeline. They had almost reached it when a figure stepped out from behind a gaily painted oak to block their path. His fur was matted and dirty and his eyes were wild.

"Hardulph!" Ruby slammed to a halt and turned back, only to find Charlotte standing in the mouth of the tunnel.

"I told you I would not be humiliated," said Hardulph.

"Do the job I paid you for," said Charlotte. "Finish them."

Ruby squeezed Fillan's hand as Hardulph advanced. Her plan had been a good one. Until now.

CHAPTER 30
Endgame

Ruby scoured her brain for ideas as Hardulph stalked towards her and Fillan, but found nothing. She knew she couldn't outmanoeuvre him a second time. Behind them, she heard the click of Charlotte snapping another clip of bolts into her crossbow.

"Make this quick," said Charlotte. "Or do I have to deal with them for you?"

"Don't tell me how to hunt," Hardulph snapped.

Ruby and Fillan stood back to back.

"As soon as we're dead, she'll kill you," said Ruby as Hardulph loomed over them.

"Don't listen to her," said Charlotte.

Hardulph didn't answer, but he didn't strike either.

"It's true," said Fillan. "She can't afford to leave any

witnesses. Including you."

A thoughtful growl worked its way up Hardulph's throat. "She might try," he said. "But I will not leave this hunt unfinished."

Ruby reached back and grasped Fillan's hands. "Sorry," she said.

"Me too," he replied. "We almost made it."

She shut her eyes and waited for the killing blow.

Instead, she heard running footsteps and a yelp of shock from Hardulph. She opened her eyes again in time to see a flash of red streak across her vision. It darted into Hardulph's path, only to roll out of range as he lunged at it. The red figure sprang upright and, with a jolt of astonishment, Ruby saw their face.

"Roselyn! What are you doing here?"

"You sent Hans Zimmerman to fetch help, didn't you?" Roselyn somersaulted over another swing of Hardulph's claws.

"Help from Akako."

"Well, who do you think called me?"

She pirouetted aside as a burst of crossbow bolts punched a hole in a nearby balsa wood tree.

"I don't care how many of you I have to kill," said Charlotte. "I'm ending it here." She shifted her aim to Fillan and squeezed the trigger. At the same instant, two more red blurs cannoned into her, and the shot went wild.

"A little help?" said Akako as she and Voss tried to grapple the weapon from Charlotte's hand.

Fillan rushed to help them, and Ruby was so distracted that she almost missed the flash of white fur as Hardulph leaped at her. She ducked the attack and sprang up beside Roselyn.

"I can't believe you thought *I* was the killer," said Roselyn. Hardulph snapped at her, and she danced backwards out of reach.

"I didn't know what to think," Ruby replied, vaulting over a fake bush as Hardulph turned back to her. "You stole the deeds for the training centre."

"I didn't know anything about the training centre," said Roselyn. "I wanted Marceline's player assessments. I was afraid she planned to drop me as captain."

"Is that all?" said Ruby.

"Isn't that enough?"

More crossbow bolts thudded into the scenery as Charlotte threw Fillan off her and unloaded half a clip at Akako and Voss, who sprinted for cover. "Just kill them already!" she screamed at Hardulph.

"Can you guys handle Hardulph?" said Ruby. "Leave Charlotte to us."

"Got it," said Roselyn. With a sharp whistle, she called Akako and Voss to her side. "We're running interference," she said. "Three-way interweaving split, stay on your toes and don't let him near Ruby."

"Yes, Captain!" chorused Voss and Akako. The three of them began orbiting Hardulph, running in different directions, weaving closer to him, then out of reach. He snarled and snapped, and made for Ruby, only for Voss to yank hard on his tail.

"Rubbish!" she laughed as he turned in anger.

"I've seen stray dogs with more talent," said Akako, running up and tapping him on the shoulder. He whirled around again, but she was already out of reach.

Ruby ran to Fillan and helped him pick himself up. "Now it's our turn," she said. They plunged into the treeline together as Charlotte renewed her pursuit.

"Whatever this plan of yours is," panted Fillan, "you need to make it happen quickly."

"Just a little further," she said. She looked back. Sure enough, Charlotte was following.

They stumbled through water traps, over nets and under low-strung ropes, until they reached a small clearing surrounded by bushes of silk flowers. She pointed Fillan across it, and was almost to the cover of the undergrowth on the other side when she fell.

"Oh no!" Fillan pulled with all his might, trying to set her back on her feet, but it was too late – Charlotte burst into the clearing.

"Enough," she wheezed, pointing her crossbow at them. "You're finished."

Ruby put her hands up. "You can't kill us all," she said. "Me, Fillan, the rest of the team. There are too many of us."

"I'll do whatever it takes to put a stop to this monstrosity that Alarick and Marceline were building," Charlotte replied.

Very slowly, Ruby got to her feet. "Is that really how you see the new training centre?"

Charlotte laughed. "How can you not? The proof of Alarick's great redemption, so we can all pretend that he'd changed? It's a sick joke."

"But he wasn't pretending," said Ruby. "I know what he did was wrong, but he really wanted to make amends."

"Not to me," said Charlotte. "I couldn't let him become a hero."

Ruby swallowed. "You put the poison on the flowers."

"It was so easy," said Charlotte. "Nobody questions where you go in this place if you're a reporter. Once your little press conference broke up yesterday, I headed for reception. I'd seen the flowers on my way in, and it only took me a moment to add the Lupix Venenum. I was back before anyone even noticed I'd gone."

"Then you planted the poison in Marceline's locker," said Ruby. "You wanted to frame her, but you got the wrong bag."

Charlotte nodded. "You were never meant to be part of this, but I couldn't let you and Fillan run around the city unchecked. What if the police caught you and got to the truth?"

"So you set Hardulph on us," said Ruby.

"For all the good he did," Charlotte replied. "Never send a wolf to do a woman's job."

Despite the weapon pointed at her head, Ruby's anger rekindled. "He almost killed Marceline."

Charlotte merely shrugged. "She chose Alarick over me, so she deserves to suffer."

The last shreds of sympathy that Ruby had felt for Charlotte vanished. "I see," she said. "Thanks for making that so clear to me. And to the audience at home."

A note of doubt crept into Charlotte's voice. "What are you talking about?"

Ruby folded her arms. "You can come out now, everyone."

The bushes rustled, and from behind every one, a reporter emerged. Photographers appeared from behind trees, and the clearing was briefly illuminated by the stuttering starbursts of flashbulbs.

"This is Franz Rust for WNBR," said one reporter into a radio mic. "What you've just heard is the stunning live confession of Charlotte Grimm, the *real* Tooth and Claw killer. We had the whole case back to front, folks!"

Charlotte backed away, waving the crossbow around the circle of faces. "Stop it," she said. "You can't."

"We already have," said Ruby. "It's over, Charlotte. You lost."

"Never," she spat. "Hardulph! Stop messing around with those kids and help me!"

Her words were drowned out by the low throb of airship engines, a moment before the shadow of the great craft fell over the group.

"Drop your weapon and put your hands up," barked an amplified voice.

Charlotte turned and ran straight into the solid bulk of Detective Breck, flanked by two squads of police officers. They already had Hardulph cuffed and muzzled, and as Charlotte stared at them in disbelief, Breck brought a hand down and swatted her crossbow to the ground.

"Charlotte Grimm," he said, "you're under arrest."

CHAPTER 31
Five Months Later

It was a damp morning early in the new year, and Ruby walked arm in arm with her parents, kicking through half-melted snow to the gates of the paper mill. They stood open, allowing a parade of workers and vehicles in and out; the mill was clad from head to toe in scaffolding, and the din of construction could be heard across the Narrows.

Roselyn, Voss and Akako waited with their families outside the perimeter fence, breathing steam like chimneys and stamping their feet against the cold. Ruby ran to them, and the team went into a huddle as the adults exchanged pleasantries.

"I can't believe we're finally here," said Ruby.

"Don't get too excited," said Roselyn. "It's not finished yet."

"Yeah, but it's our first look inside," said Voss. "Don't pretend you're not curious."

"Definitely," said Akako. "It's going to be great."

Ruby hoped so. The last few months had been a seemingly endless ordeal of police statements, court appearances and, once Charlotte and Hardulph had finally been put behind bars, newspaper interviews. Through it all, she and the others had been doing the slow and painful work of stitching the broken team back together. It hadn't been easy, especially for Roselyn, whose father had narrowly avoided a jail term for illegal gambling. So today felt like a reward for their efforts – a glimpse at a brighter future together.

"You're all here!"

They broke from their huddle to find Fillan standing beside them, wearing a yellow hard hat.

"Welcome to the Mill – the most advanced Tooth and Claw training centre in the country. I'll be your guide today." He caught Ruby's eye and grinned. "If you'd all like to follow me?"

As he led the group across the lumber yard, Ruby muttered an apology to her parents and sped up until she was walking beside him.

"I wasn't expecting to see you here," she said. "What's going on?"

He chuckled. "All will be revealed."

They stepped inside the building to find it transformed. All the machinery had been cleared out and the old roof replaced with glass panels, flooding the space with light. It looked much bigger now than it had that terrible night when Hardulph had attacked. And sitting in the middle of it, as solid and immovable as a machine herself, was Marceline. She was remonstrating with a team of builders, who all hurried away at her command. Satisfied that her orders were being carried out, she turned her wheelchair to face her guests.

"About time," she said. "I've been waiting to show this place off. Pretty grand, eh?"

The parents, aunts, uncles and brothers all oohed and aahed appreciatively.

"It's looking good, Coach," said Voss.

Marceline beamed. "Better than good. I'm setting up a wheelchair league, so the whole place has to be accessible. The architects are tearing their hair out." She laughed. "The last of the new electrics are going in this week, plumbing's due next month, and the refectory will be outfitted by spring."

"Refectory?" said Ruby.

Fillan doffed his hard hat. "That's where I come in. All these teams are going to need somewhere to eat, and the

Running Pup will cater to their every need."

Ruby grabbed him by the shoulders. "You're getting your own place?"

"Isn't it brilliant?" he said. "I've already worked out the house specials. And it's going to have a great vegetarian menu."

She pulled him into a hug so fierce, she lifted his feet off the ground. "I can't wait."

"When will this place be open for business?" asked Akako.

"End of the summer, even if it kills me," said Marceline.

Ruby set Fillan back on his feet and looked around, picturing the space clean, brightly painted and full of new training equipment. She exchanged an excited grin with her parents. "We'll get a whole season to train here before next year's final."

"About that…" said Marceline. She exchanged a furtive look with Roselyn.

"What's up?" asked Voss.

"I've decided to step down from the team," said Roselyn.

There were gasps from all assembled.

"But why?" said Akako. "I thought we'd put all the hard stuff behind us."

"We have," said Roselyn. "But this place is the start of

something new, and the team needs a new direction. Besides, I want to help Daddy get his business back on track, and I've already found a *lot* of efficiency savings to be made."

Mr Brandt blushed. "She's quite a taskmaster."

"That's only half the story," said Marceline. "I'm going to need help whipping the next generation into shape, so Roselyn's agreed to work part-time as my coaching assistant."

"You'll still be seeing a lot of me," said Roselyn. "But the Reds will need a new captain. Marceline and I have discussed it, and I think it should be you, Ruby."

Ruby looked around the circle of faces. Her father appeared to have tears in his eyes. "Why me?"

"Why not?" asked Fillan. "Teamwork, leadership, strategy and instinct. I can't think of anyone better."

Ruby blushed. "That's very kind of you, and I'd love to accept…"

"Then it's settled—" Marceline began, only to be cut off by a gesture from Ruby.

"I'd love to accept," she said. "But not yet. I've still got a few things to learn." She turned to Akako. "I think it should be you."

Akako looked as if Ruby had just pulled a crossbow on her. "Me? Why?"

"For all the reasons Fillan just gave," Ruby replied. "You've got my vote."

There was a moment of awkward silence before Voss raised her hand. "And mine."

All three of them turned to Roselyn. "Fair enough," she said. "Mine too. What do you say, Coach?"

"Good choice," said Marceline. "Congratulations, Captain."

There were cheers, and Akako's family promptly lifted her onto their shoulders for a celebratory march around the mill floor. As the festivities continued, Fillan took Ruby's arm and drew her aside.

"I'm amazed you turned it down," he said.

"If there's one thing I've learned, it's not to get caught up in my own hype," she replied. "But I'll tell you what I do want."

"Let me guess. Roast beef sandwich with all the trimmings?"

She laughed. "You read my mind."

Look out for another giant murder mystery from P.G. Bell...

It's not every day a dead giant falls from the sky and destroys your village. But meadow-witch Anwen is even more shocked when she realizes he was giant royalty – and he was murdered.

Determined to solve the crime, Anwen and trainee sorceress Cerys are transported by beanstalk to the giants' palace. In this world they are smaller than mice, which means they can use their perfect spy-size and witchy skills to track down his killer. But how can you investigate a murder when you risk being squashed by your suspects?

Read on for a sneak peek...

The giant was big. His feet straddled the western entrance to the village square, while his head blocked the road leading out of it to the east, forcing Anwen and Eira to make their way through the surrounding fields to get from one end of the body to the other.

The closer they got to the giant's head, the more apprehensive Anwen became. She'd seen dead bodies before, of course – one of the most important services a Meadow Witch could offer was preparing the dead for burial – but she'd never seen a giant up close. No living person had. She'd heard plenty of horror stories, though – of their bloated faces and jaundiced, warty skin. Of their crooked tombstone teeth, perfect for grinding human beings into jelly.

So it was a bit of an anticlimax to discover, when they rounded the giant's shoulder, that he actually looked quite normal. His face was narrow, his skin smooth and his lips slightly parted, revealing a neat row of teeth that shone like pearls. If it wasn't for his deathly pallor, he could have been asleep.

"Take a good look at our giant," said Eira. "What's the most interesting thing you notice?"

"His clothes?" she asked. "They're really fancy."

Eira nodded. "Certainly, the finest I've seen in a good many years," she said.

"So he's rich," Anwen said. "I wonder who he was."

"That's one of the questions we've got to answer," said Eira. "And as quickly as possible."

"What's the rush?"

"There hasn't been any contact between the human world and the giants since the war ended," said Eira. "Both sides signed a treaty – the giants stay in their world and we stay in ours. No exceptions."

"So how did he get here?" asked Anwen.

"He must have fallen through one of the thin places," said Eira. She peered straight up into the sky, shielding her eyes from the sun. "Gaps that lead from their realm to ours."

"So the thin places are all up there?" Anwen pointed upward.

"Exactly. That's why most people call the giants' realm the Sky Kingdom."

Anwen squinted at the sky, half hoping to see a collection of giants staring back at her, but it was blue and empty. "Are the holes invisible?"

"Until you stumble into them," said Eira. "Which is what I *had* assumed happened to this poor fellow."

Something about her grandmother's tone made

Anwen turn to her. "But?"

"But," said Eira, "that was before I got a good look at him. And there's something wrong."

"Apart from him being dead, you mean?"

"It's a question of *how* dead," said Eira. "I've worked with cadavers all my life, and this man does not look like he passed away within the last hour."

Anwen looked at the giant again. Yes, his skin was smooth, but it was also slightly waxy, and she knew that dead bodies got like that after a day or so, if you didn't keep them cold. "Maybe giants' bodies work differently?"

"Maybe," said Eira. "But I want you to make a careful note of everything we see here. Sooner or later, someone official is going to start asking questions, and I want to make sure we have some answers for them."

Anwen nodded, suddenly businesslike. She scribbled down a summary of all the things they had discussed, then turned a page, sat down in the grass, and made a sketch of the giant's profile. It seemed like a sensible idea to keep a record of his features – people asked her to do that at funerals sometimes, as a keepsake of the face they would never see again.

When her sketch was complete, she got up and dusted the grass from her bottom. "I'm going to go round and draw him from the other side too," she told Eira, who was inspecting the stitching of the giant's collar. "In case he's got any distinguishing features or anything."

"Good idea," Eira said. "Come back and find me when you're finished."

Anwen kicked through the long grass and poppies as she made her way around the top of the giant's head.

Will anyone up there in the Sky Kingdom miss this face? she wondered, reviewing her sketch as she walked. Drawing someone always made her feel closer to them, and she realized that her view of the giant had shifted in the last few minutes. He was no longer just a thing that had crashed down into her life, but a person. A problem, yes, and a total stranger. But a person, at least.

"I hope I don't have to bury you, though," she said to the fallen body. "That would be a lot of work."

She reached the middle of the field and sat down with her back to the stream, ready to start her new sketch. That's when she looked up at the giant's face and saw the wound.

It was small but serious – an ugly bruise just above his eye, speckled with a few drops of dried blood. Anwen sketched it quickly, her sense of disquiet growing with every stroke of the charcoal. Something about that wound was wrong.

By the time she snapped her notebook shut, she knew what it was.

"It's on the front of his head," she told Eira as they stood together examining the wound fifteen minutes later. "But he landed on his back, so it can't be an injury caused by the fall. It must have happened in the Sky Kingdom, before he fell through the thin place."

Eira nodded. "I've always said you've got a good eye for detail, if you'll only learn a little patience. What else can you tell me?"

"He hasn't sustained any other injuries," said Anwen. "I asked a family of field mice to check his scalp over, in case there was another wound hidden by his hair, but they didn't find anything."

"Good thinking," said Eira. "Anything else?"

"His injury isn't fresh. I can't be sure, but it looks a few hours old."

Eira's expression was grim. "At least twelve. Which confirms my worst suspicion."

"What's that?"

"That this giant's death was no accident, and he didn't fall into our world by mistake. The blow to the head killed him sometime last night, and then his body was dumped here."

"You mean…" Anwen left the question unspoken.

"Yes," said Eira. "This was murder."

ALSO BY P.G. BELL:
All aboard for the bestselling
TRAIN TO IMPOSSIBLE PLACES
Adventures!

"Rollicking entertainment."
The Sunday Times

"Great fun!"
Philip Reeve, author of *Mortal Engines*

When Suzy hears a strange noise in the middle of the night, she creeps downstairs to find a train roaring through her house. But this is no ordinary train. This is the magical delivery express for The Union of Impossible Places.

Whisked onboard by a troll-boy, Suzy's world is turned upside down when she's asked to deliver a cursed package to a fearsome sorceress. And when the mysterious package begs not to be delivered, Suzy discovers the fate of the Impossible Places might just be in her hands...

ACKNOWLEDGEMENTS

As always, this book wouldn't have happened (and wouldn't be half as good) without the input of a lot of talented people. So if you enjoyed it, please direct your praise to my editors, Foyinsi Adegbonmire at Feiwel & Friends, and Sarah Stewart at Usborne; as well as to my ever-brilliant agent, Gemma Cooper. They all had a hand in shaping the world and tone of this story, and I'm extremely grateful to them.

Of course, the only reason I'm able to spend weeks on end holed up in my office bashing out words in the first place is thanks to the patient support of my wife Anna and our two boys. I'm very lucky to have them.

I'm also lucky to have the input and wisdom of my friend Claire Fayers, and the unfailing encouragement of the Write Magic sprints crowd, including Jules Aspinall, Annaliese Avery, Carol Christie, Catherine Friess, Sam Gale, Ian Hunter, Carolyn Nicholson, Kate Walker and far too many others to name here.

Finally, to all the young readers I've met over the past year – thank you for your questions, your ideas and your enthusiasm. You make this job a real pleasure.

ABOUT THE AUTHOR

P. G. Bell is a native of south Wales, where he was raised on a diet of Greek mythology, ghost stories, and *Doctor Who*. He's had all sorts of jobs over the years, from lifeguard to roller coaster operator, but has always wanted to write stories for a living. His books include the *Train to Impossible Places* series and *The Beanstalk Murder*.

He lives in Wales with his wife Anna and their two children.

@pgbellwriter
www.pgbellwriter.com